FURST AND MAYNE

BOOK I

THE CASE OF THE PHANTOM SCARFACE KILLER

A Work of Fiction By

eM. Douglas Wade

DEDICATION

*I dedicate this novella to my loving
and ever-patient wife, Barbara.*

ACKNOWLEDGEMENTS

First and foremost, I acknowledge my friend and editor, Kate Johnston of Kate Johnston Creative Services, for helping me make this project as print-ready as possible. Kate, you are indeed a star in the craft.

To my professors and instructors at Southern New Hampshire University, I thank you for your genuine interest in my education and your firm but gentle nudging when needed. When I thought I might fail in my quest, you gave me the confidence to see my way through. I count you among my friends.

I would be remiss if I did not mention the friendship and support of the Wiggin Memorial Library writers' group members, both past and present, for their enduring support and encouragement over the years. I have missed our meetings these past long COVID months.

Next, I give special acknowledgement to the staff of the London Library for their assistance in helping me get the historical facts correct for this novella. The staff was exceptionally kind and accommodating.

I am also most thankful to The Conan Doyle Estate for allowing me to use characters found in the Sherlock Holmes canon. I appreciate their thoughtful response to my requests, and I pray that I have treated their characters with the respect they so richly deserve.

Finally, I am so grateful to my wife, Barbara, for her love and understanding, especially through my years in the Master of Arts degree program and throughout my writing of this novella. She has the patience of Job and the heart and Wisdom of Solomon. I love you, babe.

-eM.

Disclaimer

This novella is a book of adult historical fiction. It is intended solely to entertain. In its writing, the author has not wished to offend any person, living or dead, nationality, city, organisation, or manufacturing concern. The author apologises if he has in any way affronted any or all.

TABLE OF CONTENTS

CHAPTER 1
INTRODUCTIONS, AN OFFER, AND AN ACCEPTANCE

For your consideration, dear reader, with the kind assistance of my devoted sister and able secretary, the widow Mrs Rebecca Atkins, Becky, I've dictated the events of the past many years as best I remember them. I fear the cruelness of time may dull my mind, and I will no longer be able to recall the details tomorrow as clearly as I remember them today. It is vital for you, reader, to understand in detail how I came to meet my dear friend and partner and our first case—one of murder, theft, and intrigue.

Let us begin. It was early Friday evening of 15 September 1882 when Becky introduced me to the extraordinary man with whom I was to share many adventures and dangers. His name was Siderus Furst.

I had only returned to England for mustering out of the Army two weeks before. Moreover, I had only returned to London two days ago. Upon my arrival home, Becky insisted I lodge with her at least until she put her late husband's affairs in order. Thomas, "Tommy" Atkins, then a corporal in my regiment, had not only been my brother-in-law, but he had also been my closest friend. Two years ago, a well-placed Boer sharpshooter's bullet had ended Tommy's life in South Africa during the fierce and bloody fighting on Majuba Hill.

Becky operated a boarding house, a well-maintained three-floor structure in the Marylebone area at the corner of Dorset and Baker Streets, near Paddington Street Garden. She said that with six suites and few lodgers, there was ample room for her pensioner brother. I offered, and she appreciatively accepted my assistance for whatever she needed, cleaning, a bit of painting—doing whatever I could to help her run the establishment. We had agreed my labour would be sufficient payment for room and board.

She would not hear of higher rent until I found more practical and profitable work.

Becky and I were engaged in pleasant conversation and enjoying our evening's tea and biscuits in front of the warmth of the parlour fireplace when I heard someone descend the staircase. I could tell from the sound of the heavy footfall upon the steps and the slightest of regular "clicks" that someone was a large man wearing an articulated prosthetic appendage—an artificial leg. Stepping into the room with a well-worn black felt hat in hand, the man begged to speak.

'Please pardon my imposition, Mrs Atkins, and to you, sir, but I shall be going out, and I do not know precisely when I shall return this evening,' the man said, slowly surveying the room as if he were considering something and everything. 'If you would be so kind as to have a sandwich or two, and perhaps some black coffee, brought to my room upon my return, I would be most grateful.'

'Of course, Mr Furst. I'll see to it, that is if it's not *too* late. As I must arise early, I must abed early, as well.'

'I see. Yes, of course, that is fair enough,' Mr Furst replied.

I arose from my chair to face the singularly striking man. His clothing was of an uncommon cut—definitely not Savile Row. It was more of what I would surmise might be worn by fashionable American gents. Appearing to be a man near my age, forty, or thereabout, muscularly built, nearly twelve stone, he stood over six feet in height. His blonde hair hinted at a slight trace of silver. His eyes were of a piercing blue slate, and his moustache, turning up slightly at the ends, was neatly trimmed to just beyond the edges of his mouth.

'Oh, Mr Furst, may I introduce my brother, Abaddon Mayne. "Baddy," as I call him, is just back from—'

I cleared my throat, rudely but forcefully cutting my sister off from giving additional information about me to the man. After all, we were meeting for the first time. I felt no need to provide the stranger with my life's story. I extended my hand to him, and he graciously accepted it with a firm grip. Without releasing my hand, he spoke.

'Siderus Furst at your service, and it is my distinct pleasure making the acquaintance of a former sergeant, is it, of Her Majesty's 60th Rifles? You have recently returned from service in South Africa, I presume. Did I deduce correctly?'

Taken aback, I recovered my hand from his.

'Here now,' I sputtered. 'How did you know?' I glanced at Becky. Had she spoken to him about me?

Becky shrugged, apparently not knowing what to say.

'Ha!' Throwing back his head, Mr Furst laughed sardonically. 'So, I *am* correct.'

'Yes, but how did you *know*?' I asked.

'It is nothing, really,' he said. 'I call it "ODDS." Not at all a parlour game, I assure you. It is merely a matter of Observation, Detection, Deduction, and Solution.' With what I would call exaggerated self-confidence, he continued. 'First, I noticed your carriage is erect and proper, and you give the impression of one who is confident in himself. That bespeaks to me, 'seasoned soldier.' Your boots are Bluchers, standard issue to the British Army, enlisted men, and non-commissioned officers alike. However, I notice yours are well-kept and spotlessly polished. That bespeaks of your being a sergeant.

Your facial complexion and the back of your hands appear quite darkly tanned, though your sister's face and hands are not. Therefore, you must have recently seen service in either Africa or India. Finally, your stick, the one resting on the mantle above the fireplace, the polished silver pommel displays the Roman numerals "LX" and the initial "R." That was your regimental number, was it not? And since I know of no British regiments of that numerical designation currently serving in India, I surmised you served in South Africa with the 60th Rifles.' He asked smugly, 'Did I get any of that *incorrect?*'

'Amazing! All correct, Mr Furst.' Still somewhat flustered, I said, 'I took the "queen's shilling" many years ago. I'm recently retired, a former colour-sergeant, from the Rifles, and I receive a tidy but small pension for the four- and twenty-years o' faithful service what I gave to the regiment and the Crown. But, enough about me. Now, let me do a bit o' deduction about you if you don't mind. I'm a little bit "ODD" meself,' I said, half-smiling.

'I do not mind at all,' said Mr Furst. 'But, please do not make jest of my method. It is quite sound and well-proven, I assure you. Would you care to make a game of it, say a shilling to me for every incorrect guess you make, a shilling to you for every correct one? Go ahead and give it your best try if you dare.'

I nodded my agreement to the wager. 'First off,' I started, 'you're an American.'

'Ha, that is nothing,' Mr Furst countered. 'Anyone could deduce that from my speech and dress.'

'Please, do let me continue,' I insisted. 'As I don't detect any recognisably distinct dialect, I would place your origin as either New York State or Pennsylvania, nearer Philadelphia, I believe.'

'Hmm. Go ahead, if you are able,' Furst coaxed.

'Oh, yes, I'm *quite* able. Next, I would say you've been either an army or a naval officer, a graduate o' one o' your country's academies–Class o' 1864, I believe. Further, from the slight bulge in your coat, just below your chest on your left side, I would venture you're carrying a firearm. And from that observation, I would surmise you are now either an inquiry agent or a criminal. If it's the latter, sir,' I said sternly, 'Mrs Atkins and I *must* demand o' you to quit your lodging here at *once!*'

'Bravo! Mr Mayne,' said Mr Furst, ' Excellent use of your deductive skills. 'Yes, it is evident I am American. I hail from Pennsylvania, Harrisburg, to be precise. I was an Army officer and a United States Military Academy graduate at West Point, New York, Class of 1864. I was a detective for several years, what you fellows call an "inquiry agent," most recently with the Pinkerton National Detective Agency. I am now in private practice and work for clients who need and are willing to pay handsomely for my exceptional abilities and skills. Therefore, I hope you and Mrs Atkins will allow me to continue my stay here.'

I looked at Becky, who'd remained seated. Her expression was one of perplexed yet entertained amazement. She nodded her assent to Mr Furst and me.

'Mrs Atkins agrees that you may remain in your suite if you wish,' I said.

'Thank you, both. Please rest assured I shall not cause any trouble while I am a guest under your roof. Now, Mr Mayne, let me try to detect how you deduced all that out about me. For the life of me, I do not know how you determined from where I hail in America. Regardless, you noticed my academy class ring and observed the year displayed upon it in raised numbers. Correct?'

I nodded, wondering if this strange man would pay off his wager.

'As far as the handgun is concerned,' Mr Furst continued. 'I carry one in a special holster below my left armpit. Since there is no law against my carrying the piece in your country, I am no criminal.'

'Now, regarding my deductions, what you have stated, in fact, *is* how I deduced,' I said. 'I must admit, however, I have some knowledge o' your land. With me as his aide—our war office dispatched my colonel and me, a mere corporal at the time, to observe a battle or two during your civil war in 1863 and report our findings to Horse Guards. Ashamedly, Britain was contemplatin' whether to offer its support to the Confederated States. I must say I'm so very proud that our queen, God bless her, chose as she did to stay out o' the conflict. You know, England abolished slavery by an act of Parliament in 1833.

'Now, about your place o' origin. I've, o' course, heard the dialects o' your southerners, and I've read in American novels about how your quaint New Englanders speak. Your dialect is neither. Therefore, I surmised Pennsylvania or New York as your home. Further, from what you say, you spent years in both.'

'I will give you credit for all. I must say I am quite impressed with your powers of observation and deduction, Mr Mayne. I know of few men who have them. Here are the four shillings you have won from me fair and square.'

I grasped the shillings from Mr Furst's open hand. 'I wouldn't have been much o' a sergeant had I not had the power o' observation,' I said, promptly pocketing the coins. 'Why, in fact, I wouldn't have been much more than a common *ranker* without good peepers and a properly functionin' brain behind 'em. It seems to me, Mr Furst, that we both share the power o' observation.'

'Quite so. I agree with you to the fullest, Mr Mayne,' Mr Furst said. 'Say, I require a good, dependable guide and assistant, one who knows the lay of the land and who would know how to handle himself in the clinches, so to speak. I planned to advertise in one of your London newspapers, but on second thought, you are the very appearance and essence of the man I would seek and more. What do you say, Mr Mayne, would you care for such employment?'

'Well now, that would depend upon how much the work paid and what you'd be in need o' me doin'. I am in want o' employment; that much is true,' I stated. 'How long would you need my services?'

'Fair questions, Mr Mayne, fair questions all, indeed. First off, I am willing to pay at the rate of one of your English pounds each week and expenses to start in advance. Regarding how long I would need your services, that would depend entirely on how quickly I can conclude my business here. Roughly, I would say, three or four weeks, perhaps longer, might do it. You would need to accompany me wherever I may want to go, anywhere in London or elsewhere within Britain, for that matter. Further, you would need to be available to me at any hour needed. You would be my guide and right-hand man. Does this appeal to you at all, or should I look elsewhere?'

'Blimey, such generosity, Mr Furst! Might I speak about your offer with Mrs Atkins?' I asked. 'In all fairness to her, sir, I have agreed to help out here with her boarding house.'

'Oh, Baddy, go ahead. Take the job,' Becky said, nearly pleading. 'I know you don't care much for being an on-call chambermaid. It would do you good to be out o' the house amongst the folk—your acquaintances from times past. Besides, it'll be for *only* a few weeks at most, Mr Furst says. Then you can return to ol' number 12 Dorset and help me out if you wish. Think o' what you could do with a few extra bob in your pockets. Will he be safe and all legal-like doin' this work, Mr Furst? I couldn't bear losing him.'

'My dear Mrs Atkins, why he shall be as legal and as safe as I. He and I shall seldom be apart when we are on the job. Please do not worry. Besides, I believe Mr Mayne to be a man who can take care of himself. In fact, I am certain of that.'

'Yes, yes, I'm sure o' that, as well. But, just the same,' Becky said, 'Baddy's all I got left in this world now.'

'I do understand, Mrs Atkins. Well, Mr Mayne, what do you say?'

I first glanced at Becky, who nodded her smiling approval, then down at the threadbare Persian carpet, thinking of what I could do with the extra money to help my Becky, and finally into Mr Furst's waiting and welcoming face. It would be good, I thought, to be physically active again. I extended my hand once more and said, 'I'd say we have a deal, Mr Siderus Furst. When do we begin?'

Grabbing my hand in both of his, he said, 'Excellent, Mr Mayne, excellent. A deal it is. We begin in earnest tomorrow morning. Say, I was just going out for a bit of evening air and perhaps a little imbibement. What say we tonight celebrate our venture with a pint or two of London's finest beverages? I saw a pub around the corner when I first arrived. Would that do?'

'Ah, the ol' Lion's Claw,' I said. 'Aye, that should do quite nicely. Allow me to gather up my coat and hat from my room upstairs. Mind you, I'll be just a moment.'

Though I had left the room, I could hear Becky speaking to Mr Furst. Her words, though muffled, drifted up through the ceiling vent and into my bed chamber above. When I heard Becky mention my name, I lingered a while, despising myself that I should listen in on their conversation. It was about the war and what I had experienced in

South Africa. I knew my sister loved me, and I felt her concern, but I could not share with her the horrors of battle and how Tommy had died.

'Mr Furst, please try to get him to speak about the war if you can,' Becky asked. 'He's been through so much, and yet, he's been so silent about it. I know he left the Army, his home for so many years, because o' my husband getting killed. Further, I know Tommy's death was not Baddy's fault. Them pinning that medal on my Baddy only made things worse for him, I think. Do you know about the Victoria Cross, Mr Furst? Well, our queen awarded Baddy that medal. The Army told me it was for his courageous actions on Majuba Hill. That's in South Africa, you know, where my Tommy's buried.'

'Mrs Atkins, I am so very sorry for the loss of your husband. I all too well know the horrors and losses that are brought about to many by war. As such, I believe time and your patient love may help your brother confront his tortured thoughts and feelings more than by any imprudent prodding I might attempt. Later, in a few months or a few years, he may even begin to speak of them to you, but in his own way and in his own time. I beg you to allow him his opportunities when he is ready.'

'Bless you, Mr Furst. You seem like a kind and wise man. Thank you for your comforting words to a grieving widow and concerned sister.'

'Not at all, Mrs Atkins, not at all.'

'Well, Mr Mayne,' Mr Furst said to me in a somewhat perplexed manner as I returned to the parlour. 'You went to get your hat and coat, yet here you have returned to us empty-handed. Is everything all right? Should we try for another night, perhaps?'

'I-I don't know what to say. No, I'm quite keen on the outing. In fact, I'm lookin' forward to lifting a pint or two with you, Mr Furst. I'll be right down.' I was embarrassed, poked up, by the appearance I must have made, giving Mr Furst the impression I was absentminded, at best, and this after our duel of deductive powers only moments ago. Reliving the war, even for a moment, had thrown me off balance, but I was determined to soldier on. As quickly as I had left, I was back again—this time with my coat and hat.

'Ah, that is better, is it not?' Mr Furst said, winking. Then, to my sister, he promised, 'I will not have him home too late. Good evening, Mrs Atkins.'

'Good evening, Mr Furst. Baddy, look after Mr Furst, won't you?'

'I will, ol' girl,' I called over my shoulder as I closed the door behind Mr Furst and myself.

CHAPTER 2
FRIENDLY ALE AND A CHANCE MEETING

We stepped into Dorset Street, as busy as it would be on any Friday night in Marylebone—carriages, cabs, and people going in all directions, all in a hurry. Mr Furst commented about the smell in the air, the odour of raw sewage, the musky scent of wet cobblestones, and horse urine, but it smelled as sweet as ever to me. Ah, Marylebone! It was good to be home. The streetlights were glowing, and there was something about the night. Maybe it was just my being out and about with this strange American gent, an ex-soldier like myself.

'Although it goes without saying, I will say it anyway—it is obvious your sister cares deeply about you, Mr Mayne. I hope you are not offended by my being so familiar with you, it being that we have just met, but family is a subject so very dear to me.'

'No, I'm not offended in the least, Mr Furst. Becky seems to worry about me needlessly, though. Ever since my return from South Africa, she's been doggin' me about what happened there and about my leavin' the Rifles. She seems overly concerned about what I'm goin' to do with the rest o' my life. I know she means well, Mr Furst, but sometimes a bloke needs to think it all out on his own—and there are things wot happened over there I don't dare share with her.'

'Yes, I know precisely what you mean. The same happened to me upon my return home from my war. My father, a wonderful man, was a widower when I was young. Although he was curious about my experiences, he knew to leave it alone. When I was ready to talk about it, I took him aside and told him things I am certain he would rather have not heard. Still, I was a much lighter man, so to speak, for having taken down that heavy burden I had been carrying. I was better able to move on with my life, and I believe sharing what I had kept so long to myself helped bring my father and me even closer.'

'I see what you mean. Perhaps, someday—ah, here we are, sir, the Lion's Claw. Mind you, the clientele here's not what you might call genteel, Mr Furst.'

'I am not worried, Mr Mayne,' he said, appearing to suppress a sly grin. 'I have you to protect me, now, don't I?'

As we entered the noisy, crowded room, the barely breathable air was full of cigarette and cigar smoke. I noticed Mr Furst systematically scanning the room. He appeared to be quickly analyzing every soul in the pub, one person after another, each in turn. The friendly pub looked no different from the many other times I had frequented it— the same proprietor, though a bit older and fatter, and many of the same regulars were there. There were men from all classes—fancy gents, factory workers, an assortment of businessmen, skells, the well- to-do and the ain't-doin'-too-wells—all enjoying their drinks of choice. One old fellow, passed out across a table in the corner, had "enjoyed" his drink too much, perhaps, I thought.

'Do you do that everywhere you go, Mr Furst—the lookin' around?' I asked.

At first, he didn't acknowledge my question. He continued surveying the room as if he were looking for a particular individual. 'Hmm? Well, you never know when you might see someone whom you have met somewhere before. It is a habit of mine that has served me well and kept me alive on several occasions. Shall we find a table? Ah, there is one over in the corner near that gentleman who, from all appearances, unless I am deceived, is one of your English "inquiry agents."'

'I'll grab us a couple o' pints,' I said as Mr Furst strolled to the empty table. 'The first round is on me,' I yelled over my shoulder as I walked to the crowded bar. Waiting for the keeper to pour our pints, I observed an extraordinary occurrence from the bar. Mr Furst got up from our table, walked over to the gentleman he had mentioned to me, briefly said something, handed him a card, and received one in return. He walked back to the table as I approached with our drinks.

'Made a new friend already, have you, Mr Furst?'

'Interesting fellow, that. We exchanged cards and a few words,' Mr Furst said as he read the card. 'An unusually likeable gentleman for, as I surmised, a private detective. I think you might like him, as well, Mr Mayne.'

As the man left, he and Mr Furst politely nodded to each other.

'Well, what's so unusual and interesting about the bloke?' I jokingly asked as Mr Furst handed the card to me. It read *SHERLOCK HOLMES, Consulting Detective, 221b Baker Street, NW1, London.*

'Sherlock Holmes? I've never heard o' him. And a consultin' detective? Consultin' with who, I wonder,' I said, still staring at the card.

'Well, you *have* been out of the country for a while. Therefore, I do not doubt that you do not know the man's name. While in the service of Pinkerton, I heard mention of a man in London with uncanny deductive abilities. Mr Sherlock Holmes is that man. As far as with whom he consults, I think it is obvious he consults with your Metropolitan Police.'

'He consults with Scotland Yard, does he? Ha!' I spoke. 'He sounds to me as if he's quite full o' himself—consults with the Yard, indeed.'

'I believe him to be everything he claims to be and more,' Mr Furst said, calmly sipping his ale. 'However, I do not think we will need his services. We *shall* need to check in with Scotland Yard tomorrow, though, if we are going to be able to get on with our work in earnest and if you are to earn your "keep."'

'Mr Furst,' I replied, 'just what's it that you expect to find in London? You haven't told me what you've been tasked to do and by who. Or shouldn't I ask?'

'Mr Mayne, you shall know all in due time, but for now, know whatever happens, we *must* not fail in our work.' Mr Furst drained his mug. 'Drink up, my friend. Your next pint is on me.'

Mr Furst and I stayed at the Lion's Claw, drinking ale and talking about life in London, until near closing time. I did most of the talking. Though a patient listener, Mr Furst was very reticent about his life in America. When we finally left the pub, the weather had turned damp and foggy. Luckily, it was only a short walk back to number 12 Dorset-Street.

I turned the key in the lock. I opened the door, and we stepped into the dimly lit parlour.

'Dear Becky has gone off to bed, I see,' I said as we each quietly made our way to the comfortable chairs in front of the cooling fireplace. 'Look here, Becky's made up a couple o' sandwiches and a pot o' coffee, bless her. Have a seat and help yourself to your late dinner.'

Mr Furst sat and poured coffee into the two cups Becky had provided.

'The coffee may be a bit on the cool side,' I said as I picked up one of the roast beef sandwiches from the tray on the tea table between the two chairs.

'I have drunk many a cup of cold coffee in my days and nights on the battlefield, as I am sure you have as well, Mr Mayne. This coffee is perfect. Please convey my compliments and thanks to your sister for her kindness.'

'I certainly will do that, Mr Furst. Earlier, you spoke o' your father. Does he still live in Harrisburg?'

'My father is dead, Mr Mayne,' Mr Furst said, without adding more.

'Oh, I'm so sorry. I didn't mean to meddle in your personal affairs.'

'Do not worry, Mr Mayne. You are not meddling. Father was a wonderful man who died too many years before his time. I think about him every day I continue to live and—' He stopped talking and took a bite of his sandwich.

'Do you have brothers or sisters?' I asked.

'No, it has, er, *had* always been just Father and me. And you, Mr Mayne? Besides Mrs Atkins, do you have a family, or has your Army life prevented you from having a family besides your brothers-in-arms?'

At that moment, it struck me hard that Mr Furst must be still grieving the loss of his father—perhaps as I still mourned the loss of Tommy. Like me, Mr Furst seemed outwardly private, even stoic in his emotions.

'No, Mr Furst. I never had any brothers or any other sister, just my Becky. The closest I had to a brother was Tommy Atkins. I knew him since we were lads. He grew up an orphan in the streets. Our mum and dad treated ol' Tommy as if he was one o' their own. They passed years ago whilst Tommy and I was both on duty in India—first Mum and then Dad. I guess the ol' man just couldn't stand livin' without his sweet companion. I would swear he died o' a broken heart. Poor Becky had to deal with all o' that by herself, and then when Tommy was killed...'

Mr Furst did not speak. For a moment or two, he seemed lost in thought. Perhaps he was thinking about his father and home, or maybe he was simply feeling the effects of the ale as he stared unblinking into the flickering coals.

'Yes, yes, tragic, quite tragic,' Mr Furst said after what seemed like several minutes. 'Well, I suggest that we turn in. Tomorrow promises to be one filled with activity. We must pay our respects at Scotland Yard and let your fellows there know what we are about. We do not wish to run afoul of them, now do we?'

'Ah, no. I agree. That would not advance your investigation or whatever you and your client hope to accomplish.'

We bade each other a good night, and I cleared the china from the parlour before retiring. In bed, before drifting off to sleep, I thought about what Mr Furst had said about me not having a family life. The Army had been my life, and Tommy Atkins had been right there with me, shoulder to shoulder and soldier to soldier, through it all until the end. No, no, as much as I missed Tommy, I wouldn't have changed any of it for a wife and kiddies. I still had my Becky, and she was all the family I needed.

Chapter 3
Breakfast and then Scotland Yard

Early the following morning, I made my toilet, got dressed, and went downstairs to breakfast. To my surprise, Mr Furst was already at the table. Becky was refilling his cup as I walked into the kitchen.

'Good morning, Becky and Mr Furst. I trust you slept well, sir, and are none the worse from last evenin's activities.' I gave Becky a peck on her cheek, which was my habit from the old days. She mussed my hair a bit, a practice of hers, as well.

'Baddy, sit yourself down,' she said. 'I'll get you your eggs and toast. Mr Furst was tellin' me about meeting an important gentleman at the pub.'

'What? So, *he* says,' I retorted as I poured a cup of coffee, which overflowed into my saucer. Perhaps the thought of that conceited popinjay of an "inquiry agent" at the pub thinking himself more intelligent than the Metropolitan Police put me on edge.

'Thank you for asking, Mr Mayne. Yes, I am feeling fit, and thanks to Mrs Atkins' cooking, I am replenished. Once you have eaten *your* breakfast and drained your saucer, we shall hail a cab for Scotland Yard. Agreed? As your fellow Englishman, Geoffrey Chaucer, so aptly put it, "tide and time wait for no man."'

How quaint a phrase, I thought as I buttered my toast and took a sip of coffee. Mr Furst, however, had already left the kitchen and the house. I heard the front door open and then close again.

'Becky girl, I'll see you later. It appears that Mr Furst is anxious to get his day started, either with or without me.' I took one last sip of coffee, pocketed my toast, and rushed out of the house. It was a sunny morning, but the cobblestones still glistened with the evening dew or the carriage horses' urine. It was difficult to tell, except for the effects upon the hairs in the nose—urine, it was.

'Mr Mayne, how grand of you to join me,' Mr Furst said, half-glancing in my direction. I barely spied the twinkle in his eye as he turned away to face the street. 'Shall we?'

I raised my hand to the first hansom that passed. It stopped, and we got in.

'Scotland Yard,' I said to the driver. As Mr Furst appeared content to remain silent during the ride, I slipped the piece of toast from my jacket pocket and finished my breakfast.

'How far is Scotland Yard from Dorset-Street?' Mr Furst finally spoke.

'Oh, I'd say it's just under ten miles.'

'And what do you suppose the fare will be for the trip?'

'According to my calculations,' I offered, 'the fare should be near a crown. That is, about five shillings.'

'Fine. You pay the fare. Keep track of our expenses, and I shall settle up with you at week's end.'

'Is that how it's goin' to be, then, Mr Furst? I pay for the fares and all?'

'That *was* the agreement. You must remember the deal we contracted in your sister's parlour. We shook hands upon the agreement. Do you not remember?'

'Well, *I'll* be.'

'Just as you took the queen's shilling when you enlisted in the British Army, so have you done in the Lion's Claw last evening with mine,' Mr Furst said, all serious-like.

'How's that, then?'

'As you were looking elsewhere, I placed one of my shillings in your pint mug. You should have observed my doing so. It is apparent to me that you missed it,' Mr Furst then beamed as if he were pleased with his cleverness.

'What? You mean the shillin' what I *did* observe you dropping into my drink, the one what I saw in the bottom o' my mug, the one what I snagged with my teeth, spit into my hand when *you* weren't lookin', and stored in my trousers—the one what's *now* in your coat's right pocket?'

Furst's smugness evaporated from his face as he placed his hand into his pocket to discover the presence of the otherwise contentious shilling.

'Outstanding, Mr Mayne. Outstanding, indeed! What do you say, shall we call a truce?'

'If you say so, Mr Furst. If you say so,' I replied, though I believed he would continue testing me until he was thoroughly satisfied with my abilities.

Several minutes later, the cab jerked and rocked to a halt.

'I believe we have reached our destination. Please pay the man, Mr Mayne,' he said as he stepped down into the street outside the courtyard of the Metropolitan Police Headquarters.

I stepped down, also, and paid the cabbie the owed crown piece and tuppence more.

'Thank you, gov,' the cabbie said as he drove off.

The bluebottle on duty at the door inquired as to our business. I told the constable, 'We're needin' to speak with an inspector. It's official police business.' He let us pass without much ado.

Once we entered Scotland Yard, the desk-duty sergeant directed us to the Criminal Investigation Division upon our query. There, we asked for any available inspector. We were soon escorted into an office and announced to the smallish, ferret-faced, familiar-looking gentleman sitting behind the cluttered mahogany desk. Although it had been years, I believed I knew the man. The shiny brass nameplate confirmed it on its front, proudly proclaiming *Chief Inspector G. Lestrade*. I couldn't believe my eyes!

'Well, I'll be!' I said with great surprise. 'It's ol' "Granny" Lestrade from the ol' neighbourhood!'

Standing, the obviously flustered runt of a moustached man sputtered, 'It's "Inspector G. Lestrade."' We shook hands, but his was as moist as today's fresh catch. I wondered what Mr Furst would have to say about such a handshake.

'I *am* sorry, old chum. Mr Furst, this is my boyhood mate from the old days, Granville Lestrade. Tommy and I used to call him "Granny" because o' his actin' older than his years and *other* things.' I did not call up the *other* things. Granny's present demeanour demanded I refrain from further comments on the subject.

'Please address me as "Inspector Lestrade" when we are not in more private settings,' he said as he took his seat and slowly regained his composure. 'How have you been, Abaddon, and what of Tommy Atkins? Is he still the wild one?'

Briefly, I brought my old friend up to date without going into too many details about the past twenty years or so.

'So sorry to hear of Tommy's demise, Abaddon,' Granny offered, shaking his head. 'He *was* a character.'

Changing the subject, I said, 'Please allow me to introduce my present employer, Mr Siderus Furst. This gent is the American version o' our inquiry agent. He has extraordinary powers o' observation and deduction.'

They shook hands. 'Not *another* one,' Granny said, again shaking his head. 'Well, at any rate, welcome to London, Mr Furst. May I inquire what brings you to England and our fair city?'

If the soggy greeting took Mr Furst aback, he didn't let on one bit. 'I wish you to be aware, Inspector, that I am on a case for a client whose identity he wishes unknown. Inspector, I am pursuing a man who is a murderer, an arsonist, and a thief and his accomplice. For several months, I have been chasing them across the breadth of Europe, and I now believe them to be somewhere in England—most likely in the London area. I have sworn to apprehend the pair and bring them to justice in the United States, whatever the cost.'

'I see,' Granny said, appearing unimpressed with Mr Furst's story. 'It *is* true that through the Imperial Extradition Act of 1870, there exists an agreement between Her Majesty's government and that of the United States. However, you *must* possess a warrant issued by your justice system to execute such actions. Do you possess such a warrant, Mr Furst?'

'Alas, it is a fact I possess no such warrant,' Mr Furst replied. 'The court system in the state of Pennsylvania is convinced that the primary man I seek is dead. Therefore, I must obtain proof that he is alive and continues his crime spree across Europe to secure such a document. The pair deceived the best reputable European arms manufacturers, costing their companies a fortune while getting nothing in return. I believe they will try to play their game here, in England, Inspector.'

'I see. Regardless of warrants, what are the names of these men?' Granny asked. 'Perhaps they are wanted for a crime in this country.'

'The leader's name is Simon McCreedy,' Furst said. 'But I doubt he is using that name here. I believe him to be accompanied by his co-conspirator, William Mason, who may be using an alias like "Mason Williams" wherever he goes—Italy, Germany, and France—but always the same men using the same modus operandi.'

'McCreedy, McCreedy,' Granny repeated as he thumbed through reports of recent criminal activity in London. 'No McCreedy here, Mr Furst. No William Mason or Mason Williams, either.'

'As I stated, Inspector Lestrade, they most probably will not be using their real names. And "Williams" was only one example of an alias he could be using.'

Mr Furst's tone suggested a rising temper, and my old friend, Granny Lestrade, did not help the situation with his calm, detached, and officious responses.

'I am afraid, Mr Furst, that I cannot see how Scotland Yard might be of assistance, given that you have no concrete proof of your allegations.'

Granny did not indicate to Mr Furst that he cared to hear more.

'Inspector Lestrade, I have spent weeks chasing them across Europe. Time is of the essence, sir. Please take what I have told you more seriously!' Mr Furst pleaded.

It was of no use. Mr Furst's passionate appeal would not move my old friend. He calmly looked down at his vest, brushed off what appeared to be a biscuit crumb, and then at the watch he pulled from his pocket.

'Apparently, sir, Mr Sherlock Holmes is *quite correct* in his assessment of your abilities,' Furst erupted. 'You are fortunate, sir, to have such a magnanimous consultant at your disposal!'

The two men stared daggers at each other. It was apparent to me that we'd worn out our welcome.

'Come, Mr Furst,' I said, tugging at his jacket sleeve. 'I'm certain the Inspector is quite busy and has little time for suppositions and phantom-chasin'. Good day, Inspector.' I ushered Mr Furst from the office. 'We're staying at my sister's establishment at 12 Dorset-Street if anything o' interest regardin' Mr Furst's case should come your way,' I called over my shoulder.

Granny slammed the door behind us. I was sure the glass in it would shatter. It didn't, thank the Good Lord.

'I believe I was correct in my unqualified belief the Metropolitan Police can be of no help to us, Mr Mayne,' Mr Furst said as the desk sergeant brusquely escorted us to the front door and out of the building. 'We are on our own.'

'Well, if they would've given you any help before, they certainly won't now,' I cautioned. 'And what was all o' that poppycock about Mr Sherlock Holmes and what he said about the Inspector's abilities?'

'Poppycock or not,' said Mr Furst. 'I would be certain that Mr Sherlock Holmes thinks little of the Inspector though he may not have ever said so to him. I believe that would be his logical valuation of the man's worth as an investigator, as it is mine. Come, Mr Mayne, we have much work to do.'

'Where to next?' I quietly moaned, wondering if I'd erred in my decision to work for Mr Siderus Furst.

'Why, to the city's greatest repository of knowledge, the London Library. Where else? Please be so good as to hire us a cab, and do not worry, Mr Mayne. You made the correct decision about working for me.'

How *did* he do that? I wondered. How could he know what was on my mind?

CHAPTER 4
NEXT STOP -- THE LONDON LIBRARY

I waved down a cab, told the driver our destination, and we began our rather long journey to the London Library.

'Back there,' I said, pointing my thumb over my shoulder, 'well, it was as if you were—'

'Reading your mind? Oh, Mr Mayne, it was nothing as psychic as that, my friend. I simply detected in the tone of your voice that you were questioning your decision to join me in my work. I believe that would have been the logical meaning of your *moan*. And I was correct, was I not?'

'Yes, that *was* what I was thinking. Dash it all, Mr Furst! That was quite discomforting, just the same.'

'All right, all right. In the future, Mr Mayne, I will try not to be so obvious if I should attempt to surmise what you might be thinking. I shall simply keep it to myself.'

'Thank you, sir,' I said. 'Very much appreciated.'

Aside from the sound of horse hooves upon the street, we rode for not a few miles in silence. From all outward appearances, Mr Furst appeared to enjoy the ride, looking out at the passing scenery but never making any comments. I figured then might be a good time to ask him about the case.

'Mr Furst,' I started, 'do you suppose you might share with me some o' the details o' the case?'

'Well, Mr Mayne, exactly what would you like to know about the case so that I might give you succinct answers tailored appropriately to your questions?'

'Ah, all right, then. I have learned that the man you're pursuing is Simon McCreedy, a person o' interest who may be from your home state. Who's your client? Where was the crime committed? Who was the victim? I know none o' this, Mr Furst. Yet, you want me to help you with your work. To what end, sir? Don't you think I should know more?'

'I shall not name the client for now,' Mr Furst replied. 'His name is for me alone to know. The crime, I can disclose, was committed near Harrisburg. There were two victims, both of whom, for now, also will remain known only to me. I will give you more details as we uncover the clues that will undoubtedly lead us to the apprehension of our Mr McCreedy. More than that, I cannot, *nay*, I shall not say.'

'I'm certain you're aware, Mr Furst, that you've told me little more than what I already knew.'

'Precisely, Mr Mayne.'

Finally, we arrived at the end of our journey. I paid the driver. Stepping from the cab, we climbed the five steps, entering the imposing three-story, marble-faced London Library at its main entrance. Mr Furst quickly found the librarian and asked for the reference section. The librarian pointed toward the ornately carved staircase that seemed to me to beckon the inquisitive upward.

As Mr Furst stepped off towards the stairs, I asked him, 'Would you mind if I took the time to look around this wonderful ol' building? Or would you prefer that I accompany you wherever you're going?'

'No, I should not require your assistance while we are here, Mr Mayne. When I have concluded my research, I will find you.'

When I was sure he was well on his way to research, I asked the librarian for directions to the international periodicals. He pointed toward the back of the first floor. 'Ask for Mr Smythe,' he said as I hurried to the section. Once there, I found a slight, dark-haired, bespectacled young man in a tailored suit whom I took for Mr Smythe. He was straightening piles of newspapers.

'Pardon me, sir, but do you know if there are any American newspapers amongst all o' this?' I whispered.

'My *word!* There has been *so* much interest in news from America since their war that we now have an extensive collection that is growing each day. It is all *quite* exciting!' His voice quivered, and I wondered how such a thing could excite a man. 'The newspapers,' he continued, 'are arranged by state and then by date with the most recent on top. For which newspaper are you looking?'

'I'm not quite certain, but it should contain news o' Harrisburg, Pennsylvania,' I said.

'Ah, this way, please.' I followed Mr Smythe to a narrow section where the wall was labelled *U.S. – Pennsylvania.* There, cabinets were designated by major cities such as Philadelphia, Pittsburgh, and Harrisburg, and they contained stacks upon stacks of the more recent newspapers.

Overwhelmed by what I saw, I asked, 'Is there some other location where older newspapers, say by a year or two, might be deposited?'

'Why, yes. Please, come with me. This way,' he said as he led me down a winding wrought iron staircase to a darkish lower level. 'Unfortunately, we have room down here to store only the past five years of any one periodical. After that, we burn them in our furnace.'

The room was musty-smelling, and I could see that mildew had pervaded the papers stored in the rows of overflowing wooden bins. I wondered if I was up to the task. Still, if the information I needed was down here, I was determined to find it.

'Here is the bin where we deposit the older Pennsylvania newspapers that the library is holding for imminent disposal,' Smythe said, pointing toward the dirty wooden crate stencilled, *U.S. - PENN*. 'You may search for whatever newspaper we have without needing to keep them in any order. I will leave you to it, then.'

'Thank you. You've been so very kind, young man,' I said as the assistant ascended the stairs. I pulled aside any newspaper with "Harrisburg" in its banner as quickly as I could manage. It was messy work. However, I soon saw a pattern in how the papers were stacked within the bin. There, beneath each Philadelphia and Pittsburgh daily, was one from Harrisburg—*Harrisburg Daily Patriot*.

I pulled every third paper, the *Patriot*, laying it aside for further examining, beginning with dates from a year ago. In a relatively short time, I had culled the bin of all the Harrisburg copies. Then, I scanned the headlines for any unsettled crime reported in the area, only in reverse order of date. I remembered Mr Furst had mentioned something about McCreedy being an arsonist. Therefore, amending my search, I also looked for news of conflagrations. There were several headlines of fires reported in the county, but only one was reported in the Harrisburg area. I took the paper to where sunlight beaming through the only window in the room gave light enough for me to read the small print. I read the article, hoping to gain insight into what drove Mr Furst. The fire, it said, had happened two years ago at a factory, The Furstenburg Foundry, located on the city's outskirts. Ruled as accidental, the blaze, destroying a significant portion of the facility, claimed the lives of two men, tentatively identified as Mr Fredrick Furst, the foundry's owner, and an assistant, Mr Simon McCreedy.

'Ah, ha! So, I have it!' I could hardly contain my joy at discovering the probable triggering effect for Mr Furst's "grail quest." '*Yip!*' I could barely control my excitement, but lest I alarm Mr Smythe, I quickly inhaled my enthusiastic outburst.

I read on. Further, the article said that the owner's only son, Mr Siderus Furst, of the Pinkerton National Detective Agency, Chicago, had been summoned to identify the victims. City police, however, claimed that personal effects found in the victims' possession clearly indicated their identities, and they were satisfied with their findings.

Having lost my sense of time, I had no idea how long I had been down among the newspapers and cobwebs. By now, Mr Furst must be looking for me, I thought. I quickly refilled the bin with the piles I had created and hurried back up the stairs to the library's main floor, content that I had accomplished the mission for which I had set out. Mr Furst was not within my immediate sight, so after again thanking the young man who had assisted me, I calmly strolled to the front of the building. I was about to ascend the staircase to seek Mr Furst when he suddenly beckoned to me from above.

'Ah, Mr Mayne, please join me up here.'

As I made my way up the stairs, I wondered what effect the steep stairway might have had on Mr Furst's artificial leg. I followed him to a table that held several open books.

'If I were to ask you to name for me the foremost manufacturer of small arms in all of England,' he queried, 'which would you name? Take your time, please, and give me your choice.'

'Well, that's a *simple* one, Mr Furst. Why that would be the Royal Small Arms Factory, what is located in Enfield, but a few miles from here.'

'Yes, that is what my research has also led me to conclude. I believe the factory is government-owned, is it not? We will need to tread carefully with this one.'

'Will we be going there today?' I asked.

'We will not be going *anywhere* until you have wiped the printer's ink from your hands and brushed the cobwebs from your hair. Mr Mayne. Did you have a productive "look around" while I was killing time up here?' Mr Furst acerbically asked. 'I believe we have completed what we came here to do, have we not?'

'Quite so, sir,' I said as I wiped the smudges from my hands with my handkerchief and ran my fingers quickly through my hair. 'Is that better, Mr Furst?' I asked, but he was already on the move. I hoped he would not be offended by my digging into his business. But I needed to know, if nothing more than to satisfy my growing curiosity.

'I believe we shall go now,' said Mr Furst. 'Do you think we shall be lucky and find a waiting cab outside the doors of this repository of knowledge?'

More quickly than I could imagine, Mr Furst descended the stairs with relative ease, dropping one foot after the other, each in rapid succession, each additional step accompanied by a slight "click" from his artificial leg. I nearly had to run to keep up with him.

As luck would have it, a cab *was* discharging its passenger as we left the building. I looked at Mr Furst with eyes full of amazement, I was sure.

He simply smiled at me and said, 'Let us go home.'

I thought it was odd that Mr Furst would refer to Becky's boarding house, where he simply rented a suite, as "home." Still, I filed that thought away for safekeeping.

'12 Dorset-Street, Marylebone, driver,' I said. With a jerk of the cab, we were on our way.

CHAPTER 5
A CAB RIDE AND REVEALING CONVERSATION

The cab ride back to 12 Dorset began in silence, as had the trip to the library. I'd expected as much, but I wouldn't be content until I'd disclosed to Mr Furst all I'd discovered in the library's dank and dusty storage room. I was about to speak when his voice broke the silence.

'Well, Mr Mayne, did you find all the answers to the questions for which you have been inquiring of me so doggedly?'

'Mr Furst, I believe I should begin by apologising for diggin' into the affair. But quite frankly, sir, as you have been anything but forthcoming with details o' the case, you left me no conceivable alternative if I was to learn those details quickly.' Seeing no change of expression on Mr Furst's face, I continued. 'If I've offended you by doing this, and if there's no other recourse for you, I will understand if you should dismiss me from your service, sir.'

'*Dismiss* you? Why in Heaven's name should I want to do that? Besides, it is *I* who should apologise to you. I may have appeared, perhaps, overly cautious with you. However, I needed to be unquestionably certain that you were the right man for the job—the right man to be my associate.'

His *associate*? Until that moment, I'd thought of myself merely as his employee. What an exciting surprise and turn of events this was!

'Almost any dolt with muscle and tenacity could do what I think you thought I needed in my employ,' he continued. 'On the contrary, I need someone who is not afraid to pursue things, sometimes the intangible, perhaps for the sake of gained knowledge alone—one who can think beyond what someone has told him. I believe I saw those qualities in you when we first met. You have demonstrated them to my satisfaction today at the library. I had no real reason to visit the library, as wonderful as it may be. I simply wanted to see what you might do if allowed to think and achieve independently. I am not disappointed. On the contrary, Mr Mayne, I am *overjoyed*!'

'Oh, Mr Furst, I'm not sure what to say. Only "thank you" comes to my mind at the moment.' I was thrilled to my core that Mr Furst would hold me in such high esteem as to consider me his associate.

'Please let me hear what you have learned today,' Mr Furst said. Inclining his ear toward me, he appeared intent on hearing every word I was about to speak.

'To start, I learned that, two years ago, there was a fire at the foundry what's owned by your family. Further, your father, Mr Fredrick Furst, and another man, presumably identified as Mr Simon McCreedy, perished in that fire. From what you said before, you don't believe McCreedy died in the fire. If that's the case, he must have placed some o' his personal items on the body o' the second man. Further, you must believe McCreedy killed your father and the other man and made it appear that the fire was an accident. But that's only one part o' the story, I believe. You also said that this McCreedy is a thief. For this reason, other than the murders, you have pursued him across the European continent and now, here, to England.'

'Excellent, Mr Mayne,' Mr Furst said. 'High marks to you for your efforts as far as you managed to get. However, there *is* more, is there not?'

'If I may speak plainly, Mr Furst, I believe that *you* are your *own* client. I'm correct, am I not? I'm unsure o' one point, though.'

'You have found me out, Mr Mayne. Continue,' Furst urged. A smile seemed to begin and then end as quickly. It was almost as if he knew what I would say next.

'Mr Furst, I'm uncertain whether you are out for justice or out for revenge,' I said. 'If it's justice what you seek, then I'm your man. However, regretfully, if it's to be revenge, we must part company, and I must wish you no good providence upon your quest, sir.'

'It is evident to me, Mr Mayne, that you are an honourable man who believes in "fair play" and achieving balance in the Lady Justice's scales. I do admire that quality in you. To answer your question, it is justice that I seek *if* the option presents itself to me. However, suppose McCreedy and Mason do not give me that option. In that case, revenge will bring justice to my father and his employee, Mr George Washington Selfridge, a former escaped slave, longtime family friend, and exceptional metalsmith.'

I was somewhat relieved that Mr Furst's quest was not one of revenge. Still, I was unsure what he might do once he confronted McCreedy and Mason. Would revenge end up defining Mr Furst's ultimate mission? I hoped not.

'You seem certain that this Mr Selfridge is the second murdered man,' I said. 'What makes you so sure o' this?'

'To answer that question, I must give you a rather lengthy personal family history and a short lesson in anatomy and anthropology. Since we have time before we arrive at 12 Dorset, now is as good as any to bring you up to speed. Are you up for such lessons, Mr Mayne?'

'Mr Furst, I'm no educated man, but I'm eager to learn, and you'll not find a more attentive student when history is the subject.'

'All right, then,' Mr Furst said. 'My great grandfather was Friedrich Wilhelm von Fürstenberg, a captain of Hessian Jägers. Jäger is German for 'hunter.''

'My word!' I said. 'I've heard o' them buggers. From what I know, they were fierce fighters.'

'Indeed,' Mr Furst replied. 'And these troops were the best marksmen your King George's money could buy during our first war for independence. General Washington's troops captured him and many of his men on Christmas Eve in Trenton, New Jersey. Forced to sit out the remainder of the war in a prison camp in Pennsylvania, a bachelor with little family back in Prussia, Friedrich liked the country, and many of the colonists there spoke German. After the war, he chose to stay and work in the newly formed nation. Being quite familiar with firearms, Friedrich sought and received an apprenticeship with a struggling gunsmith. He and his employer grew the business thanks to his knowledge of weapons and organisation.

'At thirty-five years of age, he married his employer's daughter and shortened his name to Fürstenberg. Shortly thereafter, my grandfather, Fredrick William Fürstenberg, was born. My great-grandparents somewhat Americanised their name to Furstenberg. A few years later, they were running the business, which now included a foundry.

'My grandfather took over the business when his father was too old to run it any longer. He hired arms designers, thus expanding the business to include custom guns and substantial government contracts. The foundry turned out muskets and cannons used during our second war for independence. Are you following me thus far?'

'Yes, I am. This is all quite fascinatin', Mr Furst,' I said, determined to follow his most educating and engaging history lessons. 'Please do continue.'

'In 1821, my father, Fredrick William Furstenburg II, was born into a family that was one of the most successful arms manufacturers in the United States by then. Father married his childhood sweetheart when he turned twenty-one, but not before changing his name to Furst. My mother was barely eighteen when I was born in 1842.

'As I grew, I apprenticed in the factory as my father, grandfather, and great-grandfather had done before him. Like them, I learned to handle weapons and became a crack-shot before I was in long pants. While working in the various factory shops, I learned about the Mexican War through stories told by veterans, now foundry workers, who had returned to Pennsylvania when the conflict had ended. Their tales captivated me. Thrilled by the stories they shared, I told my father I wanted to become a soldier and not a foundry worker. Soon afterwards, my mother passed from this world. My father threw all his efforts into raising his son and expanding the business. I continued to work with my father until I was old enough to apply for admittance to the U.S. Military Academy. I received my acceptance letter when I was eighteen. It was quite an emotional task for me, breaking the news to my father. He had had such hopes of my taking over the family business. Still, even though he was disappointed and suspected that another war was on the horizon, he bid me Godspeed and shook my hand the day I left for New York.

'As you are quite aware by the raised numerals on my ring, Mr Mayne, I received my commission as an infantry second lieutenant in the spring of '64. By then, the war had been tearing my country apart for three long years. Because I had excelled in all of my studies at the academy, I graduated near the top of my class. This honour allowed me the opportunity to request the choicest of duty assignments.'

'Bully for you, Mr Furst!' I lauded. 'You are a scholar and a gentleman-soldier! That's a combination what should make any bloke proud.'

'Thank you, Mr Mayne, for your praise. I hope that I live up to it. To continue, I chose the U.S. Sharpshooters and was promptly dispatched to Virginia to command a platoon of marksmen, mostly men from Pennsylvania, during the Richmond-Petersburg Campaign. I commanded a company by the end of that bloody work, having lost my first two commanders during the heaviest fighting. It was during a subsequent battle that I was to meet then-Sergeant Simon Patrick McCreedy.'

I sat silently, mesmerised by Mr. Furst's commentary, wondering what would come next.

'The action took place as I commanded the company on the right flank of the regiment's line,' Mr Furst continued. 'Out of nowhere, Confederate cavalry appeared and attempted to roll up our flank. A big fellow on a beautiful roan came thundering up and was about to remove my head with his sabre. McCreedy ran up and got between the rider and me, bayoneting the mount. This action, of course, threw the cavalryman, but not before he had slashed McCreedy across the face. I, in turn, drew my Colt revolver and put a well-placed round between the eyes of the surprised dismounted cavalryman. Until my leg gave out from under me, and the initial shock had passed, I had not realised that some reb foot soldier nearby had put a minie ball *nicely* into my left knee. It had literally blown the kneecap to smithereens.

Thankfully, the Confederate charge failed, and the Union won the day. After the battle, hospital corpsmen took me to a medical field tent where a surgeon removed my leg below the knee. Now, I have this,' he said, smiling briefly and rapping on the artificial limb with his academy ring.

Mr Furst continued his account. 'McCreedy, whom I thought at the time to be dead, was removed to a hospital where he underwent an incredible surgery. Much later, I learned the sabre blow had crushed a portion of the front of McCreedy's skull, and from its severity, the wound should have been fatal. Miraculously, the doctors were able to attach a piece of silver plating over the damaged skull, and then they sutured the scalp.

'After being released from the Army hospital, I returned to Harrisburg, my father, and my family's foundry. I did not see McCreedy again until the day he walked into the factory's office looking for me. I almost did not recognise him. His face was severely disfigured. A jagged scar ran from his forehead down the right side of his nose across his mouth and ended at the bottom of his chin. His forehead showed a deep crevice that distorted his right eye socket. I am confident his looks would have frightened most men, women, and children. Like so many returning from the war, he needed work. My father asked me if he should hire him. Given that he had saved my life on the battlefield, I gladly gave my wholehearted approval to the employment of my old war comrade.

'He began work as an apprentice in the casting shop. Within a short time, liked by many of those with whom he worked, McCreedy made friends with designers and casters alike, including George Selfridge. McCreedy and I did not see much of each other in social settings. Because of his disfigurement, my friends were not comfortable being around him. He either kept to himself or was content socializing with his workmates.

'About that time, my father experimented with advanced designs in weaponry—weapons with a high rate of kill, semi-automatic and automatic weapons. Of course, Gatling had already created a rapid-fire gun. The Union used this weapon in our civil war. As you may recall,

Japan used it in the Boshin War, and England, in your own Zulu War.'

'Yes, it was a most terrible but effective weapon,' I said. 'But in the heat of battle, as you know, a soldier wants all the killing power what he can get his hands on. After the battle, when you've time to look around, you see what terrible slaughter you've done to win it. The Gatling at the hands o' an experienced gunner can be the instrument to bring hell to earth—there's no denying, Mr Furst.'

'Indeed,' Mr Furst said. After several seconds of what I'd say was him recollecting scenes of battlefield carnage, he continued. 'However, some of my father's designs were to be the first fully automatic weapons in the history of modern warfare. In my estimation, the use of them by any country would spell disaster for those on the receiving end. I truly believed that the designs were far too advanced for humanity. My father and I argued about this on several occasions. Like you, I had seen the slaughter on the battlefield. He had not. Still, he would not see reason. When I failed to convince him to abandon the course, he was so intent on, I felt I must leave the company.'

'What did you do after that?'

'I left Harrisburg and my family home and sought employment with the Pinkerton National Detective Agency in Chicago, Illinois. I was always interested in solving puzzles and following clues, and I learned a new trade at Pinkerton's in just a few years. That was not before Father had built the prototypes of the semi-automatic handgun. It was magazine-fed and held fifteen rounds of special hollow-pointed, nine-millimetre ammunition propelled by new smokeless gunpowder. I am carrying one of those prototypes with me today, a gift from my father. The second prototype disappeared, along with its design plans and plans of other sophisticated weapons that my father and his designers had conceived but not yet built. Almost everyone connected with the case believed everything in the design shop had been destroyed in the fire. I did not.'

'My word!' I exclaimed. 'I read that the authorities called you in to identify the bodies o' your father and the other man.'

'Oh, yes, I was called in, but the Harrisburg police had already made up their collective minds, if you can call them that. The two bodies were badly burned. There were mostly bones, fragments of cloth, and unburnt items such as buttons, McCreedy's watch, and other objects of personal significance said to have belonged to McCreedy. I identified my father's remains right away. You see, he had lost his right index finger in a drop press accident when I was about sixteen.'

I was amazed at how casually and emotionally detached Mr Furst recalled the events of the fire, especially the murder of his father. I wondered if it was the professional investigator who was talking, or was it a man who had lived with the events so long they no longer affected him, at least outwardly?

Mr Furst continued his account. 'The other body, however, I told the authorities, even though it was approximately the same build and appeared to be wearing McCreedy's clothes, was *not* that of McCreedy. They would not listen to me, and instead, a Detective Sergeant named William Mason, the chief investigator of the Harrisburg Bureau of Police, whom, strangely, I was never able to meet, closed the case.'

'How was it you were so certain the other body wasn't that o' McCreedy?' I asked.

'Secondary to the fact that the skull of the other man in the fire showed no sign of the sabre cut and silver plating McCreedy's surely would have had, was that the skull was that of a Negro. As I am sure you are aware from your duty in South Africa, Negro skulls are shaped differently from those of white men."

"I never noticed such things, Mr. Furst. I was too busy tryin' to stay alive!"

"Quite so. Regardless, the physiognomical differences are especially noticeable in the eye orbits, nasal apertures, bridges, and sills. Further, George Selfridge had a gold tooth, unusual for most Negroes. I remember that the tooth was quite prominent on the bottom of his lower jaw. The skull of the second man was missing the tooth that should have been in that place. It seemed obvious to me that whoever killed Father and George also removed George's gold tooth.'

'My word!' I said. 'And you pointed out all o' that evidence to this Detective Mason without causing him to investigate further?'

'As I said, I was never able to meet Mason, as he always seemed otherwise occupied elsewhere. Instead, I spoke with other officials connected to the case. I remember that it was quite strange with Mason. With him, it was an apparent, inescapable conclusion the two bodies were undoubtedly Father and McCreedy. When I pressed the officials about George and his whereabouts, they told me Mason's theory was that George had stolen the gun prototype and plans and set fire to cover the theft and the murders he had committed. What also rings odd to me is that the police did not try to find George Selfridge, the supposed murderer, arsonist, and thief. Further, if the fire supposedly destroyed everything, how did Mason know about the prototype and the plans?'

'From what you've told me about Mason,' I said, 'I would wager he is somehow in league with McCreedy.'

'Mr Mayne, if you could find someone foolish enough to take your wager, you would most probably be the winner. About a month from the day Mason closed the case, he was reported as having left the Harrisburg Bureau of Police. No one saw him again. Regardless of what I considered crucial evidence, I could not get his successor to reopen the case, no matter how I pleaded. With nothing else for me to do, I returned to Chicago and my job at the agency.

'McCreedy's facial disfigurement would have made him easily spotted at train, coach, or ship ticketing offices by anyone who might have been searching for him. I suspect Mason may have served as McCreedy's frontman for gaining transport to wherever he might have run.'

'Where would he have run?' I asked. 'And what could he have had in mind for the gun and plans?'

Mr Furst replied, 'At first, I thought McCreedy's idea was to sell the advanced plans to the highest bidder, regardless of country of manufacture. However, after telegraphing such reputable American arms manufacturers as Colt, Gatling, and Remington and discovering that they had not gotten any such offer from anyone, I was obliged to rethink my original hypothesis.

'I called upon the Pinkerton organisation for intelligence support. My contacts there reported that a man identified as Mason had bought two one-way steamer tickets to Genoa, Italy.'

'Genoa?' I asked in bewilderment. 'Why on earth would McCreedy want to travel to Genoa?'

'That baffled me for a time as well until I realised that Genoa is the closest port to Brescia, which, my friend, is home to the world-famous Italian family-owned arms manufacturer, Beretta. Taking an extended leave of absence from Pinkerton's, I travelled to Philadelphia, where I might secure connecting passage to Genoa. I swore I would catch up to Mason and, hopefully, McCreedy in Italy.'

'I take it you were unsuccessful in Brescia.' I was on the edge of my seat as I waited for the next bit of Furst's incredible story.

'Not entirely. I had indeed missed snagging the pair. However, I got a seed of an idea of what McCreedy's game might be. Through an interpreter, I learned from a Beretta family spokesman that Mason, calling himself "Mason Williams," had gained an audience with a couple of their designers, demonstrated the gun prototype, and gave them a brief glimpse of a portion of the plans for the other advanced weapons. So impressed were they with the gun and the prospect of securing the schematic drafts that they advanced Mason several million Italian lire on the promise that they would receive exclusive complete plans for all the weapons. They received nothing for the investment they had made. Mason, and presumably McCreedy, had most likely disappeared into the thin air of the Italian Alps.'

'Had Beretta no recourse in the matter?' I asked. 'Couldn't they have gone to their authorities with their claim?'

'Alas, they had no recourse, I am afraid. The family had neither a contract nor receipt of their payment. They had no proof that such a fantastic weapon existed, let alone plans for the more advanced weapons. They had lost their money and had gotten nothing in return.

'The Beretta family offered me a hefty reward if I captured Mason and returned their money to them. I refused their bounty but promised to apprehend the thief, or thieves, in time. So far, I have failed them.'

Feeling the cab jolt to a stop, I looked to see where we were. 'I see we've arrived back at 12 Dorset,' I said. 'I'll pay the driver. Perhaps you might continue my "history lesson" over dinner tonight?'

'Perhaps, Mr Mayne, perhaps.'

CHAPTER 6
DINNER AND CONVERSATION

Dinnertime came. I was helping Becky with the table setting and slicing the delicious-looking and delicious-smelling roast leg of lamb she'd prepared when Mr Furst joined us. He'd spent quite some time in his room after we returned from our trip. I wondered if his leg was bothering him, or perhaps it was his recalling the terrible circumstances of his father's murder and his failure to catch the murderers. I decided that I wouldn't ask. If he wanted me to know, I surmised he'd tell me in good time.

'That smells most appealing,' Mr Furst said as he stealthily picked a bit of meat from the bone.

'Here, now, Mr Furst,' Becky said, smiling. 'There'll be none o' that. I do believe you're quickly proving to be as bad as my Baddy, with his bad habits and all.'

'I am sorry, ma'am,' Furst said, 'but I simply could not help myself. I have had nothing to eat since our early breakfast, and I am near the point of vanishing from lack of sustenance.'

'Ah! Baddy and I could tell you stories, Mr Furst, o' the days on end when our family had precious little to eat— with no meat and only a single potato to split between the four o' us,' Becky said. 'Yet we survived, as can be witnessed by our very presence here today.'

'I will not deny that I lived a life of privilege in our home in Pennsylvania,' Mr Furst said as he pulled out Becky's chair to seat her at the table. 'There was always enough food to spare and to share with our workmen and neighbours. No one we knew ever went without the necessary items they worked so hard to acquire. America is truly the land of opportunity.'

Becky thanked Mr Furst for his gentlemanly act and then inquired, 'Are you a religious man, Mr Furst? We always ask the good Lord's blessing on our dinner meal.'

'That is a fine custom, Mrs Atkins, though not one with which I was brought up,' Mr Furst said as he sat. 'Please, please do not deviate from it for my sake.'

I prayed, 'Lord, we ask thee to bless this bounty for our bodies' needs and bless this home and all those what dwell within it. Amen.'

'Amen,' Becky and Mr Furst repeated in unison.

'On our carriage ride from the London Library, Mr Furst and I was discussing the case in which we're now engaged, but we was unable to finish our discussion before we arrived back home,' I said to Becky. 'Shall we continue now, Mr Furst?'

'Oh, Mr Mayne, I am quite certain Mrs Atkins would be bored to tears with such a conversation. I think tomorrow would be early enough to continue—that is if you have not already heard sufficient details to satisfy your curiosity for more than one day.'

'O' course, Mr Furst,' I said, 'if you think that best. However, I would very much like to hear more later.'

'And so, you shall, Mr Mayne. So, you shall.'

'Mrs Atkins, I compliment you on your culinary skills,' Mr Furst said. 'This is such a wonderful dinner you have prepared. At this rate, I am certain I shall need to purchase new clothes before leaving London. Mr Mayne, you are quite fortunate to have such a talented sister.'

'You flatter, Mr Furst,' Becky said. 'This is but plain fare—just lamb and a few potatoes and beans that I bought from the green grocer for little money today.'

I was surprised that Becky said our dinner was "plain fare." I suspected she was putting on airs for the benefit of Mr Furst. Why she would do that, I could not begin to understand. After all, she was still mourning for her Tommy, and we had known Mr Furst for only a few days. I dismissed the notion and instead thought about what I hoped would be a continuation of Mr Furst's fantastic story.

After dinner, Mr Furst offered to help clear the table, but Becky would not hear of it. 'You're a paying guest in this house, Mr Furst. Besides, two meals are included in the price o' your room.' Laughing, she added, 'Further, there would be no deductions in your rent for helpin' the house mistress.'

'As you insist, ma'am. If you will give us leave, perhaps Mr Mayne and I will adjourn to the parlour, then.'

'Yes, please go on,' Becky said. 'After I clean up here in the kitchen and make up the spare rooms, I'll join you two later for a bit o' coffee, perhaps.'

Mr Furst and I found our two comfortable chairs in the parlour and relaxed in silence for several minutes. It was Mr Furst who broke that silence.

'Your sister seems like a fine woman, Mr Mayne. It is a pity her husband was killed in action. Please pardon my asking a possibly delicate question, but is she still in mourning?'

Mr Furst's question somewhat took me aback. Becky and the family's private business were anything but in line with why Mr Furst was in London. Besides, what bearing would any answer I gave Mr Furst have on the case? Still, out of politeness, I answered. 'Mr Furst, the whole bloody neighbourhood is still in mourning! Tommy Atkins was a fixture, a constant in a world o' seemingly never-endin' changes. He left a hole in our lives what may never be filled. His life touched many a soul.'

'Please pardon me if you think me prying. I do understand about such loss,' Mr Furst said. 'And I have told you of mine. It seems no matter how much I work and where that work takes me, I am always alone at the end of the day. Therefore, Mr Mayne, I very much empathise with the grief you and Mrs Atkins are experiencing.'

'No apology necessary, sir. I thank you for your kind words o' understandin', Mr Furst. Becky and I gladly take each day as the Lord gives it to us, and we try to use it to our best advantage. Becky keeps busy with this boarding house and has little time for social outlets. Of course, I'll be helpin' her out here once your case is solved. When Tommy was alive, we three'd been known to take in the Gaiety on special occasions. Now that he's gone, well, it wouldn't seem right somehow to go out to such a thing.'

'What in the world is that—Gaiety?'

Seeing the confused look on Mr Furst's face, I briefly explained, 'The "Gaiety" is the Gaiety Theatre in the West End. It's like a music hall or burlesque and a great place to get your blood pumpin' if you're in the mood.'

'Oh, ho! That sounds like a wonderful place, Mr Mayne. Perhaps the three of us should go there one evening—my treat,' Mr Furst said most enthusiastically.

'If you don't mind, sir, perhaps we might discuss that some other time when Becky is up to it and you've finished what you're in London to do,' I said.

'That is an excellent philosophy, Mr Mayne. May our days always be productive and our evenings peaceful.'

I nodded my sign of appreciation for Mr Furst's sentiment. Then, to change the subject, I asked, 'Are you quite certain you wouldn't wish to continue our conversation regarding the case?'

'You are the persistent one, aren't you, Mr Mayne? Well, I do like that about you. If you are fairly certain that Mrs Atkins will be spending some time on her chores, I do not see why we should not continue. However, any case-related conversation must cease once she walks through that doorway. Are we of an accord?'

'Quite so,' I agreed.

'Now, where were we? Oh, yes, I remember now.' Without even taking a long moment to collect his thoughts, Mr Furst began where he'd left off in the cab. 'There was never any actual, hard evidence that McCreedy was with Mason, but I believed he had to be the one with the plan, more of a phantom leader, the one giving orders from the shadows. I was able to trace Mason through the accounts of train station managers in northern Italy. It seemed to me that he would try his game in Germany next. With only my rudimentary and somewhat limited knowledge of the German language and an interpreter's help, I wired the J.P. Sauer factory in Suhl and the Mauser factory in Oberndorf, warning them of the possibility of Mason's fraudulent dealings. The pair had not yet contacted Sauer. However, Wilhelm Mauser replied that Mason and an unidentified man, who had terrible head and facial scars, had been there, and, yes, sadly, they had taken their deposit of one million Deutsche marks. Once I had made them aware that it was a fraud, they contacted their government, which sent out warnings to the other arms manufacturers in Germany.

'From anecdotal stories I had heard, I deduced that the pair would not try their scheme in Russia but would instead move on to France once they had realised that no other German arms companies would deal with them. From what my father told me about competitive factories, I knew Russian arms producers are scarce and sorely inadequate. Further, from personal knowledge of Russia, I reasoned that the risk of failure and arrest would have been too high for the duo to try their game in that country.

'I found that the French arms manufacturers to be so competitive and so disorganised that Lebel, Lefaucheux, and the Manufacture d'Armes de Saint Etienne, or MAS, the famous French state-owned arms company, all had allowed themselves to be duped out of several million French francs each. That was even after I had wired all of them, warning of Mason and McCreedy and their fraud.'

'Ah, those Frenchies,' I quipped, shaking my head. 'They're a breed o' their own, aren't they?'

'Quite so,' Mr Furst replied. 'I tried consulting with each French company, in turn, to gain more intelligence about Mason and McCreedy. That proved fruitless. Oddly, the French seemed more embarrassed than angry about the whole affair. I travelled here from Paris, and I believe you know the rest of the story.'

'Is it your intention,' I asked, 'to warn Royal Small Arms in Enfield? I might be able to find out the name o' the factory superintendent. I have a mate who may still work at Enfield.'

'Your friend may prove helpful, but right now, we need to set a trap to catch our rats, and we must be careful not to give them any warning, Mr Mayne. But first, we need to secure an audience with Mr John Rigby, superintendent at Royal Small Arms. I found his name in the reference books at the London Library. He has been superintendent for only these past two years, and I am certain he would wish to avoid a scandal, especially during his recent management of the factory. I suggest we wire Mr Rigby of our desire to meet with him.'

'If you'll write down what you want to send, I'll hurry to the telegraph office, what's not far from here, and have it sent right away.'

'Thank you.' Mr Furst scribbled his message on the pad lying on the tea table. 'Mr Mayne, please have the clerk mark this as urgent, with a paid response to this address.' Pulling out his pocket watch, he said, 'I doubt we will hear from Mr Rigby before morning. I am sure it is well past quitting time at the factory. But we can only try. In truth, I should have sent the telegram to Mr Rigby as soon as we returned from the library. I can only pray that was not a too serious lapse of my judgment.'

As I'd promised, I walked at a quick-time pace to the telegraph office, which was only three streets away and had Furst's message sent. Then, I returned to Number 12 as speedily as I'd left it. Mr Furst met me at the door. 'Mission accomplished, Mr Furst,' I said as I placed my hat on the rack in the hallway, satisfied that I'd assisted in the case in even a tiny way.

'Excellent, Mr Mayne. Thank you. Would you care to join me in a cigar before we turn in for the night?'

'Don't mind if I do, Mr Furst. Thank you.'

So, we settled into our respective chairs near the fireplace. The fire gave off a warm glow that was most calming to my war-worn constitution. From the inner pocket of his jacket, Mr Furst produced a most decorative silver case. Flipping open its ornately designed cover, he offered me one of the plump cigars the case held. Taking the cigar, I commented on the cover's unique emblem. Its design was that of an eagle, with wings spread, in the middle of a crest that seemed to be supported by two angels. A crown was at the top of the ornate crest. 'What a beautiful case,' I said.

'Ah, yes, thank you.' Mr Furst lit our cigars. 'This case has been in my family for generations—brought to America by my Hessian ancestor about whom I earlier spoke. I had hoped to pass it on to my son one day. However, at my current pace, I may be as old as Abraham before that day comes,' he said, chuckling.

'Don't worry about that, Mr Furst. According to our Bible, we are told Abraham was a hundred years old when his son, Isaac, was born,' I quipped.

'Hmm, yes? Well, I hope not to have to wait *that* long, Mr Mayne,' Mr Furst said as a broad smile came to his face.

We were enjoying the wonderful Por Larrañagas that Mr Furst must have purchased before leaving America when the doorbell rang. Becky, who'd only moments before finished her rounds of the suites in need of her attending and was about to join us, answered it.

'A telegram, and at *this* hour!' she exclaimed, wringing her hands, nearly spindling the small envelope she held. 'I hope it isn't bad news. It sometimes is, you know. It's addressed to Mr Furst.'

I gave the boy tuppence, and taking the message from Becky's shaking hands, I brought it into where Mr Furst was sitting. I was about to hand it to him.

'I suspect it is from Mr Rigby,' said Mr Furst. 'I really should not be surprised at his sending his reply so quickly, given what I had said to him in mine. Not to worry, Mrs Atkins,' Mr Furst said in a soothing voice. 'It should contain good news. Please, Mr Mayne, do read it.'

'*Dear Mr Furst,*' I read, '*I have not been contacted by anyone interested in selling plans for firearms. Although tomorrow is Sunday, I am very interested in speaking with you as soon as possible. Please come to Enfield at ten o'clock tomorrow morning, if convenient. Your Obedient Servant, John Rigby.'*

'Excellent!' said Mr Furst as he flicked the long ash of his cigar into the fireplace. 'Well, I suggest we finish these fine Cubans, bid adieu to this most satisfying day, and get a restful night's sleep. We must be fresh for tomorrow.'

I agreed that tomorrow promised to add yet another chapter to our adventure, and I intended to be ready for it. Becky would need to be attending services without me this Sunday. I was a little concerned about how she would take the news—me, working on the Lord's Day and all—and it would have been our first Sunday service together, without Tommy, since I'd returned home from the Army.

Chapter 7
Sunday Morning and the Enfield Trip

Sunday morning arrived as the Lord had promised. The weather was clear, and the brilliant blue sky gave indications from all outward appearances that the day would be lovely. However, as I'd feared, there was one dark cloud on the horizon, and it was floating over Becky.

'I can't believe that any sane man would need, or want, to conduct business on the Lord's Day,' she huffed, 'even if this Mr Rigby is a most important man in Enfield! And this bein' your first Sunday back home since you left the Army. How *could* you, Baddy?'

'There, there, Becky, love,' I tried to console her as I buttered my toast, but I could feel the heat from burning eyes upon the back of my head. 'As I understand it from Mr Furst, this matter may have national, as well as international significance—it could affect our country's very existence. If we can prevent fraud from being perpetrated against Her Majesty's government and her people, don't you think we should make every attempt humanly possible? Besides, I promise not to make a habit o' it, ol' girl.'

'Good morning,' Mr Furst greeted Becky and me as he entered the kitchen. 'I am so very sorry, but I could not help but hear the end of your conversation. Mrs Atkins, I am afraid I am to blame for taking your brother from you this morning. For that, I sincerely apologise, and I beg for your forgiveness. However, the meeting really cannot wait. It is of the utmost importance that we conduct it as soon as possible. Your brother's assistance will be indispensable; otherwise, I would take the meeting alone. I hope you *will* forgive me and your brother, just this one time, Mrs Atkins.'

'Well, Mr Furst, since you've asked so persuasive and gentlemanly-like, I suppose I have no choice but to give in— *just this one time*, mind you,' Becky said through a half-smile as she poured coffee into Mr Furst's cup. 'I've no idea about what you two are up to, and I suppose I shouldn't ask. But it *must* be important for you to meet about it on a Sunday. I only hope the Lord will be as understanding and as forgiving as me.'

'I pray so, as well. Regardless, I am afraid that it is *deathly* important,' said Mr Furst as he sat down at breakfast.

'Oh, dear,' Becky sighed as she turned to look into my eyes. 'Please do be careful, Baddy,' quickly adding, 'the both of you.'

I was again surprised by Becky's including Mr Furst, still a relative stranger to us, in her wishes. We three exchanged only small talk as we finished our breakfast of kippers, toast, and coffee. We spoke no more about the meeting or anything having to do with the case. Breakfast over, we said our goodbyes to Becky and left to hire a cab for our trip to Enfield. Transport was scarce at that time of day, as many good folks were already on their way to church services. Regardless, we were fortunate to hire one within a few minutes—even though we first needed to walk a few blocks to where people were de-cabbing to go to church.

Not unlike our previous outings, Mr Furst was quiet for most of the trip to Enfield. I assumed he was formulating a plan, or at the very least, how he would broach the salient issues with Mr Rigby.

'Mr Mayne, I am on unfamiliar ground, umm, here,' he said.

To me, his manner seemed quite out of character for the man. It was true; I had known him for only a couple of days, but he appeared to be so sure of himself on all occasions.

'I have known you and your sister for such a short time, yet you two feel quite familiar to me. Perhaps it is the fact that I no longer have a family that makes me feel this way. Ever since my days at West Point, I have been self-sufficient—I had to be. I have not needed to feel close to anyone except for Father. Now, with him dead, I feel a need for family ties, or if not family, then at least a close, friendly relationship.' He continued, 'Of course, I have had professional associations with those I have studied, fought alongside, or worked closely with. As you know, from your Army days, those associations, though close as they may have been, or seemed to be at the time, are not akin to family.'

'I do understand the importance o' family and personal relationships, and I agree that nothing else in this life compares to it. However, I'm unsure as to what you're askin' if anything at all, Mr Furst.'

'Please forgive my awkwardness,' Mr Furst replied. 'Lately, at night, while awaiting sleep to overtake me, I have been doing quite a lot of thinking about my future. I understand that the rebuilding of the factory is progressing at a steady pace. Its completion and the future of its sustained operation are in competent hands. I have confidence in those running the factory for me and who will keep me informed of its operations. Still, though having been owned and operated by the generations of my family, the company does not hold my interest, nor, in truth, has it for many years. When you and I have completed this case and have seen justice done, I would like to remain in England, most likely in the London area, and continue my passion—private detective work. Further, I would like to offer you a full partnership in the venture—share and share-alike. That is if such work interests you, and you would want to continue our relationship, of course.'

My mind reeled at Mr Furst's proposition, being caught totally by surprise. I had only been back in England for less than three weeks and just a few days in London. Further, I had not put much thought, if any, into *my* future. I did plan on helping Becky run her boarding house, but beyond that, nothing. I had known little, but the soldiering I had done most of my adult life had hardly prepared me much for civilian employment. Perhaps what Mr Furst offered would solve the question of what profession I might be best fitted for. I did enjoy Mr Furst's company, and the work would certainly be challenging. There was no uncertainty in my mind about that.

'As you no doubt anticipated, I'm fairly at a loss for words at your sudden proposal. I must freely admit that Becky and I are most comfortable in your presence, which I'm certain you've already detected. However, I must consider your offer most carefully in all fairness to you and Becky. It's not enough that I'm enjoying my current professional relationship with you, Mr Furst. I must be certain that such a venture would not take me away from Becky should she ever be in need o' my assistance. As her brother and her deceased husband's friend and former sergeant, what takes responsibility for his death, I must assume accountability for her future welfare. You do understand, don't you, Mr Furst?'

'Mr Mayne, your obvious sense of loyalty to those for whom you care and your admirable willingness to take responsibility for your actions are qualities that make me want you as a partner even more. Regardless, I do understand your reluctance to my sudden proposition. Perhaps, once we have concluded this case, and you find yourself better able to give more consideration to a partnership, you will favour me with your answer.'

'Thank you, Mr Furst, for your most tempting offer and again for being so considerate o' me and o' my reasons for needin' to wait to answer.'

'Yes, of course, Mr Mayne. Now, shall we give our thoughts over to our imminent meeting with Mr Rigby? I must say I *am* surprised our dastardly duo has not yet made contact with him. Regardless, I am almost certain they *will* do this, and soon. Unless I am mistaken, duping Royal Small Arms would provide the crowning jewel to their caper. Once they have completed the act, England will be too hot for them. Afterwards, I doubt very much the world will hear from them again. That is why we must catch them red-handed and end their spree before they can pull off the final fraud and disappear into criminal retirement, most likely somewhere in South America.'

'Mr Furst, how can you be so sure about their intents and their ultimate plans?'

'Because, Mr Mayne, that is precisely what I would do.'

We rode on in silence for quite some time as our ride carried us closer to our destination.

Mr Furst, though he appeared to be watching the scenery we passed, had a faraway look in his eyes. Although I should have been thinking about the meeting and how we might convince Mr Rigby to work with us to trap the criminals, I could not get Mr Furst's offer out of my mind.

'Mr Mayne, I apologise for getting into your head at such an inauspicious time. That was poor form on my part.' He appeared to have read my mind yet once again. 'I believe the first thing we need to do is to bring Mr Rigby up to date with how Mason and McCreedy have deceived the others; perhaps even give him time to contact the deceived, which will give credence to our claim. Besides, at this point, I think it would be ill-advised of me to bring up anything but the frauds. The idea here would be to convince Rigby to invite the pair, or at least Mason, to meet with him in a day or two following the approach. That would give us time enough to ensure your boyhood chum, Inspector Lestrade, will be present when the trap is sprung. If we can nab both, that would be grand. However, even apprehending one rat should, in time, give us the other, do you not think?'

'I should think we will need to put your plan into practice quite soon, Mr Furst. Here we are at the Royal Small Arms Factory, and unless I'm mistaken, that's Mr John Rigby at its entrance.'

A man, older in appearance than in action that I could discern from his agile movement from the entranceway steps to our carriage, quickly opened its door. His dress was of impeccable business attire. His thinning hair was grey, and his long, bushy moustache nearly pure white.

We stepped from the carriage. 'I am Siderus Furst, and this gentleman is my associate, a countryman of yours, Mr Abaddon Mayne.'

'Ah, an American! Gentlemen, welcome to the Royal Small Arms Factory of Enfield, the both of you.' He smiled warmly as he extended his hand to Mr Furst and then to me. 'I am John Rigby, superintendent of the works here. Please pardon my formal business attire. I am off to services following our meeting. Believe me when I say that my wife is none pleased with my taking a meeting on a Sunday.'

Mr Furst and I exchanged furtive glances at Rigby's disclosure. My mind quickly remembered Becky's frowning face when we told her about the Sunday meeting.

'However, judging from your telegram, such a meeting was imperative to make. If you please, this way, gentlemen,' Rigby said as he led us past the smart-looking uniformed and armed guard at the inner door and into an office just off the main corridor. The office was surprisingly sparsely appointed. A few heavy floor-to-ceiling bookcases sat here and there, each overflowing with thick leather-bound portfolios, most likely containing factory operations documents. A picture of dear Queen Victoria prominently adorned one wall. Several images of men, I surmised most likely prior factory superintendents, were prominently on display on another wall, along with a collection of the various firearms presumably manufactured at the facility. A dark oak desk sat nearer one corner, and a wooden swivel chair, with its back to the tall window, sat behind it. The desk, too, was covered with papers. In front of it sat two padded, high-backed wooden chairs.

Rigby motioned to the chairs. 'Please sit,' he said as he took his seat behind the desk. 'Tell me what this intrigue is all about—a matter of life and death, you say?'

Mr Furst explained in detail what those whom we sought had perpetrated against other European arms manufacturers, how it was accomplished, and by whom.

'If those weapon plans are *that* good, I can certainly understand why anyone wanting to see his country gain military superiority over other countries would desire to possess them *whatever* the price,' Rigby said, lighting a cigar. 'Would you care for one of these?' He offered the open box to Mr Furst and then to me. We both declined his offer. 'Still, it is difficult for me to believe that several of Europe's oldest and most respected arms companies could have been taken in as easily as you claim, Mr Furst.'

'As I have heard it said, Mr Rigby, the proof is in the pudding,' Mr Furst replied, gently patting the front of his jacket.

CHAPTER 8
MR FURST'S AMAZING HANDGUN

Without speaking, Mr Furst reached into the inside front of his jacket and produced the strangest looking handgun from the holster hidden beneath his armpit. I was astonished! Mr Rigby must have felt as I did when he saw it. His eyes grew large, and his freshly lit cigar nearly fell from his mouth. 'What the blazes?' He pushed back his chair and rose to his full height. His trembling hand reached out toward the gun held firmly in its owner's grip.

'Please. Not so fast, sir!' Mr Furst admonished the older gentleman. Depressing a small button near the top of the gun's handle, he released a long, flat-looking brass tube-like device. It slid out of the handle at its bottom, seemingly effortlessly. 'This is called the gun's magazine,' Mr Furst said. 'It holds fifteen specially manufactured nine-millimetre bullets, each containing the most advanced smokeless powder and a brass-jacketed hollow-pointed bullet.' He then slid back the top of the gun, which opened with a slight "click" as it locked into the open position. Finally, Mr Furst gently handed the weapon over to Mr Rigby, who proceeded to examine every minute detail of it.

Mr Rigby was in awe. 'This is the most amazing weapon I have ever seen, and I have seen many in my time.'

If a killing machine could ever be described as beautiful, this one indeed could have been termed that way. Its body looked made of nickel plate from its approximate nine-inch barrel to the bottom of its handle, which appeared to have ornately carved ivory grips. The weapon had a clean, sleek design—very different from any handgun I had seen in all my military life.

Pointing out the various facets of interest, Mr Furst stated, 'The gun, when fired, ejects its spent cartridge out of this port at the top right, while simultaneously chambering the next round into the firing mechanism, and so on. One can fire the round in the chamber's mechanism and the fifteen rounds in the magazine as quickly as one can pull the trigger. It is the world's first genuinely semi-automatic handgun.'

Rigby was still examining the gun when he paused. 'What does this say here?' He scrutinised the weapon. *'Property of Furstenburg Firearms and Foundry Company, Harrisburg, Pennsylvania, U.S.A., Model 1880,'* he read aloud. 'Hmm, American-made, I see. I have heard very little about that small gun works. However, I believe it relies heavily on your government contracts unless I have misheard. Is that not so? How, may I ask, did you come by this extraordinary gun?'

'You have heard correctly, sir. What you are holding is one of only two prototypes my father and his designers built,' Mr Furst replied. 'The other one is in the hands of his killers, who are the criminals we hope you will assist Scotland Yard and us in capturing.'

I was surprised Mr Furst had mentioned the murder of his father, given what he had said before we arrived in Enfield. However, I surmised he could not suppress the pride he must have felt in his father's feat of engineering.

'Would it be an imposition to ask to see a demonstration of this weapon?' Rigby asked.

Mr Furst retrieved the gun from reluctant hands. 'If you have a facility close by for such testing, I should be pleased to demonstrate the operation of the Furstenburg Model 1880.'

Rigby raced from behind his desk. 'Right this way, gentlemen. Right this way. Please follow me.' He led us at a rather fast pace through the deserted factory, past intricate machinery and weapons in various stages of assembly, out its rear door and onto an extended grassy area, expertly manicured, no doubt, exposed between two high walls. Beyond, an imposing earthen berm about 200 meters downrange completed the enclosed space. At defined, varying distances, someone had erected frames for targets, most probably for the express purpose of test-firing Enfield's arsenal. Rigby hastily attached paper bullseye targets at the 25-, 50-, and 100-meter distances and rushed back to where we were standing.

Mr Furst reinserted the magazine into the gun, turned the small switch that must have been the gun's safety lever, and handed the pistol to Rigby.

'Here, Mr Rigby. I have read that you, a former member of Her Majesty's Guards, are an expert marksman. Let us see what you can do at twenty-five meters.'

Smiling, Rigby gently took the gun, extended his arm toward the target, and aimed.

'The trigger requires only the lightest touch,' Mr Furst instructed.

As Mr Furst had advised, Rigby gently squeezed the trigger. Other than producing a muffled bang, the gun gave little indication of being fired. However, the closest target was in shreds. He pulled the trigger once again, and the intermediate target also shredded.

'Allow me, Mr Rigby,' Mr Furst said, taking the pistol from him. He pointed it at the most distant target and, pulling the trigger three times in rapid succession, shredded that target and splintered the target frames of the intermediate and closest distances.

'Extraordinary! Extraordinary!' Mr Rigby exclaimed.

I was speechless. Now I understood Mr Furst's reasons for wanting to ensure that no one ever mass-produced such a weapon.

Mr Furst simply smiled as he placed the incredible weapon back into its protective holster. 'Mr Mayne, retrieve the spent cartridges if you please.'

I did as Mr Furst had instructed and placed the five spent brass cartridge cases in my jacket pocket.

'I had no idea that such magnificent weapons were possible, Mr Furst,' Mr Rigby said.

'I am afraid that *this* weapon is the least deadly of the ones my father and his engineers designed,' Mr Furst said. 'Imagine weapons that could fire several hundreds of rounds in a minute. As you might now understand, the world is not ready for that much killing potential. We *must* ensure a more even balance of that power; would you not agree? These weapons are *not* the way to achieve that.'

'Most reluctantly, I must agree,' Mr Rigby nodded. 'Still, I would so much like to examine the inner workings of your amazing gun, Mr Furst.'

'That can never happen, Mr Rigby,' said Mr Furst.

'Well then, might I keep one of its rounds?'

'I'm afraid that also is out of the question.'

'Pray tell me, Mr Furst,' Mr Rigby asked, 'what would be the incentive for me to work with you in capturing these so-called criminals? Perhaps they would actually sell the plans to me.'

'The plans, Superintendent Rigby, are not *theirs* to sell. They were acquired, in truth, stolen, through their commission of a capital crime,' Mr Furst stated most firmly. 'Furthermore, I fervently believe, Mr Rigby, that you are a gentleman of principle and honour and that you know helping the police put an end to these killers' run would indeed be the right and honourable thing to do. Furthermore, I see by your ring that we are brothers in the Order of St. Adrian, and as such, you have subscribed to our creed, "brother before self."'

'Ah, yes, the Order. Thank you, Brother Furst, for your kind assessment.' Mr Rigby glanced at his ring, which depicted two severed arms, one holding an anvil and the other a sword. Then, Furst's identical band displayed conspicuously before him. 'You have a keen eye. Yes, undeniably, I must aid you in any way I can to regain your family's plans and assist the police in apprehending the scoundrels. However, should you ever change your mind about releasing those plans—'

'Superintendent Rigby,' Mr Furst replied, 'I am afraid that I would sooner see the plans in the hands of my *own* government before turning them over to another. Furthermore, I have no intention of allowing *any* government, including my own, to possess the plans. Ultimately, I must destroy the plans along with any existing prototype weapons. That *is* the moral "high road" I have chosen to take—the one I *must* take, regardless of what that might mean in lost revenue to my family's company and me, or even in the company's subsequent demise.'

'What action do you suggest I take should the blackguards contact me, Mr Furst?'

'Oh, it is just a matter of time, Mr Rigby. I believe one or both of them will indeed approach you, either in person or by telegram, and most certainly urge an immediate meeting. The greedy pair could not possibly pass up Royal Small Arms. Your establishment would be the plum in their fraud pudding. When you *are* approached, I suggest you put off taking any meeting with them by at least one day—perhaps making the excuse that your chief designer is on holiday or ill. That should allow you adequate time to contact us and for us to make arrangements with the inspectors at Scotland Yard.'

'I will do as you instruct, Mr Furst. You can be certain of that. Now, if you gentlemen are ready to leave, I will see that a carriage can take us where we need to go. For myself, I must to church, for which I am already late.'

Within a few minutes of Mr Rigby's sending word, a landau arrived at the door where we first entered Royal Small Arms. In a few moments, we three were leaving Enfield. We spent the ride to Mr Rigby's church engaged in small talk about the beautiful day and the fresh, clean air. No one spoke of the issue that Furst predicted would develop over the next few days, but I would guess that was on all of our minds.

After dropping Mr Rigby off, we continued toward Dorset Street and home. The conversation became more serious several minutes before we arrived at number 12.

'Mr Mayne, I am afraid that to solicit the assistance of the police,' said Mr Furst, 'I am going to have to eat some crow when we once again visit Scotland Yard.'

'What? What's that, you say? You'll eat a crow? Why on earth, man, would you want to do something like that, and how would such an act gain assistance from the police?'

'Oh, that is just an American colloquial idiom, Mr Mayne, meaning humiliation by admitting wrongness or having been proven wrong after taking a strong position. Moreover, whether or not I am mistaken about Inspector Lestrade's detecting abilities, I will have to convince him that I believe he is better at his profession than I first suggested and that I was in error. It grates on me to do that, but we will need his help.'

'I see,' said I, glancing out the window at the scenery while suppressing a smile. 'Well, shall we give it a go tomorrow? If you'd like, I'll gladly assist you with your meal o' crow in front of Granny.'

'Hmm? Ah, yes, your boyhood chum, "Granny" Lestrade. Mr Mayne, I would be most grateful to you if you would accompany me to Scotland Yard tomorrow, hopefully, to reacquaint with your friend, the good Inspector.'

Soon, we were back at Becky's boarding house, where we would enjoy the rest of the day in peace and quiet. The evening found the three of us in the parlour near the warming fire, with hot tea and biscuits all around. Becky and I taught Mr Furst the card game of penny-ante Brag. He was a very quick study, and after only a few hands, he let neither Becky nor me win another hand the rest of the evening. I was grateful that we played only for pennies, and I told him so.

Chapter 9

Monday Morning: Back to Scotland Yard

'I have never avoided confrontation either on the battlefield or in my personal life,' Mr Furst said as he walked, almost shuffling into the kitchen.

I thought it a most unusual greeting to Becky and me at breakfast on Monday morning and so out-of-character for Mr Furst. He always seemed so sure of himself.

'However, I am not looking forward to re-acquainting myself with Inspector Lestrade this day. I freely admit that thoughts of it gave me fits of anxiety for most of the night,' Mr Furst said. 'In fact, because of a certain discomfort in my abdomen, I am not certain I could eat more than three eggs, half a dozen sausages, two slices of toast, and a cup of coffee for breakfast.'

'That's a very good thing, Mr Furst,' Becky said, 'because you'll not be havin' any o' that fare this rainy beginning o' your day. You'll have to settle for freshly baked sweet rolls and plenty o' hot tea instead. Please be seated, and I'll pour you a cuppa. Would you care for a bit o' honey in your tea?'

Mr Furst joined me at the table. 'Rolls and tea? Hmm. Yes, I will take that honey and plenty of the rolls, if you please,' he said.

'With all the pennies and ha'pennies you took from Becky and me at Brag last night,' I chuckled as I buttered my roll, 'if you are still ravenous after breakfast, you could afford to buy a couple o' ploughman's lunches and a couple o' mugs o' ale, to boot at midday.'

'Well, we shall see about that,' Mr Furst said as he buttered his roll. 'I would most certainly be willing to do so, and for the three of us, if our meeting goes well with Inspector Lestrade this morning.'

'Did you hear that, Becky, my love? We'll be dinin' on the generosity o' Mr Furst for lunch.'

'What I heard, Brother dear, is that certain strings are attached to Mr Furst's offer,' she said, her fists resting on her hips. 'Baddy, you must make sure your little get-together with Granny goes off without difficulty, or you'll both be dinin' on last night's mutton in a stew for your luncheon and your dinner.'

There was that stern demeanour about Becky's words and posture that I immediately recognised, even though we had been apart for many years, that told me she understood the importance of the upcoming meeting. Before that instant, I had not realised how much she must have supposed about Mr Furst's mission and how desperate he needed this chapter in his life to come to a closure.

Further, for a fleeting moment, I had the improbable notion that Becky might be having compassionate feelings for Mr Furst. Could it be that the relationship between them, or at least on her part, might be somehow changing from that of landlady and tenant to something more personal, perhaps even romantic? However, I quickly dismissed the idea. How could such a ridiculous thought have crossed my mind? After all, we had but known Mr Furst for such a short time. There was no way that Becky could possibly have gotten over Tommy so quickly. He'd been dead for only two years.

Upon finishing our breakfast, Mr Furst and I donned coats and hats, bade good morning to Becky, and left the house. Shortly, I waved down a hansom, and upon my command to the driver, we were on our way once again to Scotland Yard. The falling drizzle wet the cobblestones and the road apples lying upon them.

Before entering the cab, Mr Furst took a deep breath, puffing out his chest. Smiling, he said, 'Ah, the smell of wet horse manure! It always reminds me of the Pennsylvania farm fields of my youth.'

Nothing came to my mind to reply except, 'Yes, it certainly is a lot o' fruit from a horse's arse.' This comment, I said with a sly smile. I could not tell if Mr Furst was being serious in his statement or making some kind of American joke. I took it for the latter.

We arrived at our destination and asked the uniformed door watch to direct us to Inspector Lestrade's office. Moments later, Mr Furst and I found ourselves in the now-familiar outer office of the Inspector. We had only time to notice that we were the only ones there before a gruff voice summoned us to enter.

'Ah, my old *chum*, Baddy Mayne, and his American *friend*, Mr Siderus Furst,' Inspector Lestrade said, remaining seated behind his desk, his hands clasped so tightly upon his chest that his fingers appeared to be without blood. 'Once again, you have dared come to bother the busy police inspector, I see. And after such an auspicious first meeting, to boot. What is it this time? Have you come to hurl more insults at my feet?'

'Inspector Lestrade, you have every right to be angry with me, for I spoke things to you in rage, out of my frustration, that were unkind and untrue,' Mr Furst said, his hands behind his back. I noticed the fingers on both of his hands were crossed. 'I am almost certain that Mr Sherlock Holmes must hold you and your professional detecting abilities in the highest regard. In fact, truth be told, I attest that we never even spoke of you during our brief encounter Friday night last.

The citations upon your walls, to be sure, must certainly reflect upon your accomplishments. And as for Mr Mayne's part in our unfortunate previous encounter, well, all I can say is that he speaks to me of you as if you were a brother, and I hope that you should not look upon his part in our last meeting as anything other than that of an innocent bystander. That said, would you please forgive me if I aggrieved you with my barbaric American demeanour? Further, I pray we may find common ground upon which we may begin again what I tried to establish in my feeble attempt.'

I could not help but wonder how the taste of crow must have soured on the tongue and curdled in the stomach of my employer. Still, Mr Furst's words rang of sincerity to me, and I hoped they also proved soothing to Granny's ears and ego.

At first, Granny appeared lost for words, and his face seemed flushed upon hearing Mr Furst's apology. Then, he spoke slowly and deliberately.

'Mr Furst, I have taken into consideration your natural unfamiliarity with how we conduct police work here in London and your personal involvement in the case on which you are working. I, therefore, can understand your frustration with our cautious, unexcitable, and somewhat dispassionate approach to detective work. We Scotland Yard professional criminal investigators do not and cannot afford to let our emotions get the better of us. Therefore, if it is your wish for the London Metropolitan Police force to expend its precious resources on your behalf, you must be willing to accept its absolute authority on all things regarding the enforcement of the laws of the Crown. If you are amenable to this, I accept your apology.'

I could see that Mr Furst's hands, still behind his back, were now clenched fists. Yet, his smooth words of acquiescence seemed to have a cooling effect on our host. 'I agree to your terms and wish to cooperate fully with you. Inspector, I desperately desire your assistance with my case, a case that I fear may have serious ramifications if not handled carefully but expeditiously, not only for the Crown but for the world at large.'

'Very well, Mr Furst.' Now obviously aglow with egotism and self-satisfaction, Granny extended his hand to Siderus Furst. 'Shall we begin anew?'

Mr Furst, unclenching his fists, took Granny's hand in both of his, shaking it firmly. He then asked if we might be seated. Once we had comfortably installed ourselves in the chairs facing Granny's desk, Mr Furst calmly brought him up to date on what he knew about the *suspected* murders, arson, theft, fraud, and our conversation with Mr Rigby, the Royal Small Arms superintendent. He went into great detail as to why he thought McCreedy and Mason were co-conspirators, why Mr Furst was confident the bodily remains from the fire were not those of McCreedy, and how he had tracked the pair across Europe and now believed them to be in England.

'You present a very tidy case, Mr Furst, but one which has not produced one shred of hard evidence to convince me that I should contribute assistance to you. Still, the impression you made upon one for whom I have the highest respect and to whom I owe the most considerable debts of gratitude speaks of my giving you the benefit of the doubt.'

Leaning forward in his chair, Mr Furst questioned Lestrade. 'Who, may I ask, is such an individual?'

'Why, Mr Sherlock Holmes, of course,' he replied. 'He left here just moments before you gentlemen arrived.'

'This is unbelievable! We spoke but a few words for a fleeting moment on Friday evening last at the Lion's Claw pub,' Mr Furst said.

'That's quite correct,' I added.

'Remarkable gentleman, Mr Sherlock Holmes. He appears to have the ability,' Granny said as he took a notepad from his desk drawer, 'to size up a man, almost instantly, and with incredible exactitude. It is truly extraordinary how he does that. Further, he has researched you, your father's arms factory, and the incident that happened there. He urged me to take you seriously concerning this matter.'

'When could he possibly have had time to research all that?' Mr Furst asked.

'I do not question how he does it,' Granny said, shrugging his rounded shoulders. 'I have long ago given up trying to figure out his methods. He has his resources, and that is all I know.' Then, taking his notepad in hand, he recited what was written upon it. 'These are the notes I took during my meeting with Mr Holmes.' He read a line or two and then asked Mr Furst to verify the information, add to, or comment on what he had written. The dialogue continued in this manner until Granny had covered all the items on the list in a depth that met Granny's and Mr Furst's satisfaction.

I found the process quite fascinating, but one in which I felt utterly excluded, as I had nothing to add or detract from the facts of the case as recorded. I hoped, however, that I would soon have some opportunity to contribute my abilities to the cause besides merely paying for our cab fares. Otherwise, I could not say that I was earning my wage.

Returning the notepad to the drawer from which he had removed it, Granny asked, 'You truly believe that these men, McCreedy and Mason, will contact Superintendent Rigby, then?'

'I do,' Mr Furst quickly replied.

'When do you suspect they will make contact, and what do you propose we do about it in that event?'

'Frankly, Inspector Lestrade, I am quite surprised that the pair have not made contact before now,' said Mr Furst. 'I am unsure as to why they would wait. They did not take so long to contact the other arms manufacturers. I will have to think a little harder about their reasons.'

'Yes, perhaps a reexamination of your facts may help you,' Granny said, appearing to be a little annoyed with what I perceived as a waste of his time.

'Perhaps you are right, Inspector,' Mr Furst said. 'Regardless, Mr Rigby will contact me, and then I shall contact you to inform you of the meeting date and time. Based on that, we can make a plan if you are amenable to such a course of action.'

Rising from his chair, Granny, now appearing anxious for us to leave his office, said, 'Yes, yes, that will be fine. Please inform me of your progress with your case, and I will see what my resources can do to assist.' He came around his desk and ushered us to the office door as a farmer might shoo a couple of errant geese.

'Thank you for your time, Inspector Lestrade. I will be certain to keep you abreast of any new developments—' was all that Mr Furst could say before Granny quickly closed his office door behind us.

Turning to me, Mr Furst said, 'What a strange little man. Well, shall we away to Dorset Street, collect up your sister, and take lunch?'

'We shall,' said I as we left Scotland Yard and strolled to where we could hail a cab. I was unsure why Granny had ended our meeting so abruptly, but considering that Mr Furst had no concrete evidence or proof of his allegations, I shouldn't have been surprised at how the meeting ended. Still, remembering our childhood days as "brothers of the streets," I was confident that when we needed him, ol' Granny Lestrade would be there, as he had been so many other times in the old days.

CHAPTER 10
LUNCHEON AND THE CITY TOUR

True to his promise, Mr Furst enjoined Becky and me to accompany him to the Lion's Claw for a hearty lunch at his expense. It was a short walk to the pub, and there was time to exchange only the lightest of pleasantries. At first, Becky was somewhat reluctant to be away from the rooming house for even a short time; however, Mr Furst's ever-winning personality and convincing ability won her acquiescence.

'Mrs Atkins, the rooming house will still be there waiting for your return, patiently anticipating your caring hand,' Mr Furst said. 'Besides, the morning has proven to be personally rewarding, and a promise, after all, is a promise.'

Once in the pub, the three of us found that we had the pick of tables. There were few patrons at that time of day. I didn't recognise the one or two who were there as what I would call 'regulars.' Unlike our previous visit to the Lion, Mr Furst merely glanced about the room instead of studying his surroundings. I thought that a bit odd, but I didn't give it another thought as Becky was now with us. I was more interested in enjoying the free lunch.

Once seated, Mr Furst and I ordered roast beef sandwiches and fried potatoes with onions and our pints of ale. Becky asked only for a hot pasty and a mug of tea. We enjoyed our meals and spoke little of the case.

Mr Furst suggested, 'Given that we can accomplish nothing more until we hear from Mr Rigby, you might serve as my personal London guide for the rest of the day. What do you say, Mr Mayne?'

'As long as you're paying me, I might stand on my head in the corner if you asked. There was a saying popular among the ranks in my time. It went something like this, "the Crown pays us lads the same to march as what it does to fight."'

'I have heard such a saying among our soldiers, as well. And no, no handstands will be necessary, Mr Mayne. I would, however, like to see the sights that any visiting foreigner might find interesting here in London and some that would not be on any sightseeing itinerary. I would ask Mrs Atkins to accompany us, but I know she is anxious to return to her daily chores.'

'Quite so, Mr Furst. Thank you for being so considerate. Besides, it might do Baddy good to reacquaint himself with the ol' town once again,' she said. 'There have been some changes, here and there; some good and some not so good.'

We finished our lunches. Mr Furst, for a change, actually paid with his own funds, and we walked Becky back to Dorset Street. Before parting company with Becky, Mr Furst requested that she contact Inspector Lestrade if she received a message from Mr Rigby. She agreed, and Mr Furst took her hand and said, 'Although I have serious doubts Rigby will send a message, thank you, dear lady, for your kindness.'

'Think nothin' of it, Mr Furst,' Becky said. Blushing, she gently recovered her hand from Mr Furst's. 'I'm happy to be of assistance in any small way.'

Mr Furst tipped his hat and smiled. He continued smiling until Becky was out of sight. I was unsure what to make of that, but I had other things on my mind—playing tour guide.

I hired a landau for Mr Furst and me. It was a beautiful day, and the open carriage would give Mr Furst the best possible views of the city. I instructed the driver, telling him we would require his services for several hours. He seemed quite taken with the idea that he would have steady work. I did not know how much the services would cost, but I believed Mr Furst would eventually reimburse me for it.

We boarded the carriage, and with a crack of his whip, the driver commanded the well-groomed mare to away. Moments later, we were viewing the most familiar of London attractions.

I narrated the histories and the bits of trivial facts about as many of the buildings and statues as I could remember or that were not new since my last departure from the city. We passed around Trafalgar Square and drove on to see Big Ben, the Houses of Parliament, and Tower Bridge. We passed Kensington Palace, and I told Mr Furst that it was Queen Victoria's birthplace. He seemed interested in all he viewed but appeared somewhat distant at times.

I could see that Mr Furst's attention was drawn to the giant glass palace in Hyde Park that Prince Albert organised for the Great Exhibition of 1851. I told him the event attracted visitors from across the world and highlighted the very best of the Empire at the time.

'My father was planning on taking me to see the exhibition,' Mr Furst said, 'but the demands of the foundry kept us from making the trip.' He momentarily glanced down and appeared subdued, inwardly drawn. However, as quickly as his apparent melancholy had come, it passed.

'Mr Mayne, this tour, so far, has been delightful and enlightening, to be sure. Now that you have shown me so many splendid facets of your city, I would now like you to show me the sections of the city that are *not so* splendid if you will.'

'I'm not quite sure o' what specifically you would want to see, or quite frankly, why you would care to see them.' I glanced at the cabbie. He seemed as dismayed as I.

'Well, Mr Mayne, if I am to seriously consider relocating to London and working here as a detective, even for a few months, I feel I shall need to see as much of the city as I can. The bad as well as the good. Do you understand?'

'Yes, I can understand your desire to see *all* o' the city, but Mr Furst, please, you will see the worst o' the city to the extreme! I implore you to reconsider your request for all that is good.'

'I hear the passion in your words, Mr Mayne. Further, please understand I do value your judgment. Believe me. Regardless, it is just to such places that I do desire to be taken. Shall we?'

Realising my words were useless, I commanded the cabbie, 'East end, driver. Whitechapel proper, if you will.' I settled back into my seat in silence, dreading our destination as if it were to be the very mouth of Hades.

Some minutes later, we were on Whitechapel Road and rolling past London Hospital, the imposing brick structure that served the impoverished masses on the East Side. Its massive clock at the top of the facade showed nearly half two. We continued. Mr Furst drank in the sights all around, his facial expression never changing. We crossed the intersection at New Road, and the St. Mary Matfelon Church spire came into view. No longer coated in the lime and chalk that gave it its Whitechapel name in the Middle Ages, the edifice stood, showing that reconstruction work was being done to it. There was some evidence of smoke scorching at the bottom section of the church. Perhaps, I thought, there had been a fire some time back. I told the driver to stop in front of the church so that Mr Furst and I could discuss where he might wish to go next.

'I think we should get off and walk for a while,' Mr Furst said. 'Do you not think that a wonderful idea?'

'Not particularly, no,' I said. It was too late. Mr Furst was already stepping down onto the thoroughfare and walking briskly toward St. Mary Street. 'Mr Furst, please wait a moment, won't you, sir? Driver, please drive to the corner o' Commercial and Hanbury Streets and wait for us there. I have no idea how long we shall be walking. If we don't come back, please call a constable.' I trotted off on Mr Furst's trail.

Several ragged and dirty street waifs had accosted him by the time I caught up to him. Each one asked for a penny or two in payment for a trick they could perform or assistance to the foreigner in front of them. For a moment, I pictured Granny, Tommy, and me as youngsters begging for our pennies all those years ago.

I offered each of the five boys and two girls a shilling each if they would clear our path of beggars and peddlers as we made our way toward our rendezvous with our carriage. Of course, they asked for two shillings each but settled for the single when I refused to pay more.

Mr Furst gave me a sly grin, and then, after pointing in the direction we were to travel, he stepped off as he followed the motley knot of urchins clearing our way. I trailed a short distance behind, observing Mr Furst with his ensemble.

On the corner of Great Garden and Chicksand Streets, the mob next encountered a shabby-looking elderly soul begging for whatever passersby might spare in change. He was dressed in a threadbare dark green military tunic and used a tattered busby for his coin collector, which he held out in his only hand. He was missing his right arm and leg, and he held himself as upright as he could, no doubt, using a crutch and leaning against the building.

The waifs were giving him a rough time, most probably hoping that we would part with a few more coins. Or perhaps they sought to dislodge the old soldier's cap from his hand. Mr Furst stepped in, calming the group while straightening up and brushing off the old soldier's ruffled clothes.

'Thanky kindly, guv'nor,' the old man said. 'Jes tryin' t'get a few bob to gets by, I am.'

Mr Furst nodded and asked me for a pound note.

'But, Mr Furst, you cannot possibly give money to every beggar what asks for it,' I said.

'I am asking not for this man,' Mr Furst said, 'but for me. Too often have I passed by like poor souls in my own country, torn from the effects of their service to the Union, without giving in to my "better angels." Call it a small penance for me to pay for my previous lack of humanity.'

I handed Mr Furst the note. He placed it gently into the man's cap.

'Thank you for your service to your country and your queen. I am sorry that your return from South Africa was not met with a great welcome from your fellow citizens,' Mr Furst said.

The man looked astonished, perhaps that a stranger, and a foreigner to boot, knew he had served in South Africa. I was somewhat surprised, myself. However, I let it pass by, previously exposed to Mr Furst's deductive abilities.

'You're a real gemman. You are, sir,' the beggar said and then snapped to attention as best as he could. Tucking his cap into the armpit of what remained of his severed limb, he offered as smart a salute as any I'd seen from any whole soldier.

Mr Furst also came to attention and offered the man a salute of his own, then turned and walked on. His entourage, once leading, was now following. Slowly, block by block, they faded and disappeared into the sea of pedestrians moving this way and that.

I thought it was just as well that we had rid ourselves of the rabble. We were approaching our carriage, sitting where I had directed the driver it should be.

A small, dirty-faced girl of about six or seven was attempting to sell matches to our cabbie without luck.

'Need matches, Mr Mayne?' Mr Furst asked. 'Need *all* that she has to sell?' he continued. 'If you have enough coin, please give her a shilling for each box she has.'

'MR FURST!' I protested. Still, I did as he ordered, to the surprise of the little match girl. She handed over the several boxes, then gave a cute curtsy and ran off into the crowd.

'If you don't mind my sayin' so, sir, you're a strange bloke, you are,' said the cabbie.

'Oh, I do not mind. I do not mind a bit,' Mr Furst said as he stepped onto the carriage.

Shaking my head in disbelief, I joined him.

Mr Mayne. 'Let us go back to 12 Dorset Street. Shall we? It has been a most marvel-filled day. I am anxious to tell Mrs Atkins all about it. Was it not all so wonderful?'

'Umm,' I replied.

CHAPTER 11
CITY TOUR ENDS AND TRAVEL BEGINS

As we rode back to the rooming house, I felt troubled that Mr Furst had spent so much of my money, with him squandering quite a sum on the wretches in Whitechapel. I was almost sure he would repay me for whatever I spent on his account. Still, to me, that was not the point. It was how he spent the money that bothered me. I held my tongue for as long as I could.

'Dash it all, Mr Furst! How could you give away so much money to beggars? Don't you know your generosity is like trying to extinguish a house fire with an eyedropper?' I was feeling quite proud of my analogy and was sure it would make an impression on my overly generous employer. Instead, Mr Furst countered with his argument for being charitable whenever possible.

'Oh, yes? Of course, I also know that many of the impoverished would be in London's workhouses, that is, if they were physically able to work. Otherwise, they would have to find other ways to pay for their needs. I believe many of those ragged children that we met today, or others like them who grow up in poverty, will turn to crime. Others, it is true, may turn to a life of soldiery, such as you have done, to your credit. I have seen that in the large cities of my country. Moreover, crime, I believe, begets crime. Further, I trust that we must all do our part to help those less fortunate than us. Do you not agree?' Mr Furst did not give me a chance to answer. 'And in the case of that poor maimed soldier, would you not share your last biscuit or the last drop of water in your canteen with a fellow campaign mate in need?'

'I would, indeed, sir,' I said. I could not say otherwise.

'Well, if you had looked beyond the obvious, a begging cripple, you would have noticed that the veteran soldier was a proud man, as evidenced by the cleanliness of his ragged yet patched uniform and the shine of his brass regimental numerals. Unless I am mistaken, and I do not believe that I am, his regiment was the *60th*. Was that not *your* old regiment, Mr Mayne?'

I was speechless. Mr Furst was correct. I hated to admit it, but I had missed all the salient details because I was focused on the obvious and my part in the war. His logic sounded flawless, and his seeming pureness of heart put me to shame. For a moment, I had forgotten about Mr Furst's quest for rooting out his father's murderers for justice, or was it for revenge? I thought about the old soldier and all the soldiers, many of whom were now aged and with whom I had served. As I began to think about Tommy, Mr Furst interrupted my reverie.

'You may be getting short of your resources,' he said. 'I will arrange for funds from Child's Bank, which I believe to be on Fleet Street. Is it not? Please provide me with an account of your expenditures since I began spending your money, up to and including today, plus your weekly wage for a month in advance, if you will.'

'Yes, yes, Fleet Street. Yes, that will be fine,' I said, somewhat flustered. He would pay my wage for a month when he had initially stated that the case should not take more than a couple of weeks to conclude. Mr Furst was a complicated man to read, to be sure.

'Well, I see we are back at old 12 Dorset Street once again,' Mr Furst said. He stepped off the carriage and headed for the door. I settled our fare with the driver, tipping him an extra shilling for his patience, and followed Mr Furst, who was already through the door and making his way to the sitting room.

Becky entered the room from the kitchen just as I caught up with Mr Furst. 'Well, it's about time you two men-about-town returned home. Less than an hour ago, a messenger came by with a note for you, Mr Furst.'

'A messenger boy, you say, brought a *note*?' Mr Furst asked. 'You mean a telegram?'

'No, not a boy—he was an older man. He brought this,' Becky said, holding up a folded piece of foolscap to Mr Furst. 'Not a telegram.'

'What was his appearance? How was he dressed? Have you seen him before today?' Mr Furst quizzed.

'He wore a wide-brimmed slouch hat what partly covered his face,' Becky said, 'and his clothes were plain and common, patched in a couple of spots.'

'Did he say anything to you? It is most important you remember everything,' Mr Furst continued.

'Oh, Mr Furst, he said nothing. Just handed the paper to me and left,' Becky said. 'There is one thing, though. I think I may have seen someone who resembled him somewhere on some recent occasion. But I don't remember when or where.' Thinking momentarily, she said, 'Oh, yes, now I remember. I think he was sittin' in a corner there at the Lion's Claw when we was havin' our lunch today.'

'Hmm. Very interesting. Few people in London know me, and even fewer know where I reside. Yet, I see the note is simply addressed, "*Mr Furst.*"'

'Well, open the note, Mr Furst! What does it say? Is it from Mr Rigby?' Dear reader, excitement got the better of me, I'm afraid.

'All in good time, Mr Mayne. All in good time,' Mr Furst cautioned.

Mr Furst turned the note over in his hands, examining it thoroughly before carefully unfolding the paper. He stared at what was written on it for a good two minutes before showing it to Becky and me. It read:

Wood

Charles

Hampshire

!

CAO, SH

'I will require your assistance with this, the both of you,' Mr Furst said. He read each word aloud, '*Wood, Charles, Hampshire*, an exclamation mark, and then *C-A-O, comma, S-H*. Very cryptic! Let us examine this backwards. *S-H* must be the sender. It is obvious to me that it is not from Mr Rigby. I wonder if the note is from Mr Sherlock Holmes. He is one of the few in the city who knows my name and where I am lodging in London. I gave him that information when we briefly met at the Lion's Claw the other evening. The exclamation mark may mean that the information in the note is imperative. Okay, the first two words appear to be a person's name, perhaps... *Wood* with *Charles* written underneath it.'

'I wonder if the name could be *Charles Underwood*?' I asked. 'That name sounds familiar, but I don't know where I might have heard it.'

'Excellent! If we follow your logic, Mr Mayne, the next word could be an address. Charles Underwood...over... *Hampshire*. Andover, Hampshire? Is there such a place?' Mr Furst asked.

Becky searched the bookshelf in the parlour until she located the book. 'Here it is, in the *United Kingdom Gazetteer*. There *is* the village of Andover in Hampshire,' she said proudly, pointing to the page on which the information was printed.

'If we are collectively correct in our deciphering, we now have *Charles Underwood, Andover, Hampshire*, an imperative, and the note possibly sent by Sherlock Holmes,' Mr Furst summarised. 'And since the information may be imperative, might not the letters *C-A-O* signify *Come At Once?*'

'Blimey! I must question why the sender wrote the note as it was instead o' straightforward plain writin'?' I asked.

'That is an excellent question, Mr Mayne. I can only surmise that the author, possibly Mr Sherlock Holmes himself, was afraid that someone unknown might intercept the message, thus revealing its contents to a wrong party or parties.'

'I suppose that is possible,' I said. 'Still—'

Mr Furst cut me off. '*IF* Mr Holmes is at this Andover place, we should not waste any time joining him. For whatever purpose, we shall find out when we get there. How *do* we get there, Mr Mayne?' Mr Furst asked.

'You should be able to catch a train to Andover if you hurry on to Waterloo Station,' Becky advised. 'That is where trains goin' south depart.' She took an old tin from above the stove and removed several one-pound notes from it. 'Here, take this. I'd hate to have you two found short o' funds on your adventure.'

Mr Furst and I exchanged glances.

'Oh, Mrs Atkins, I offer you my heartfelt thanks for your kindness, but I believe your brother has enough money to cover our journey,' Mr Furst said. 'You *do*, do you not, Mr Mayne?'

'Um, let me see.' I reached into my pockets only to find a few shillings and a couple of pennies. 'It appears Mr Furst's recent generosity has caused me financial embarrassment. I'm afraid that I am left with less than what we'll need, after all. And it's too late to go to your bank, Mr Furst.'

Glowing, Becky handed the notes to me. 'Mind you that you will repay every penny, Baddy.' I had never seen that side of her before that moment. But a lot of time had passed between my infrequent Army leaves home.

'Mrs Atkins, I shall repay you with interest. I assure you,' said Mr Furst. 'Again, thank you for your timely benevolence. You have saved our fledgling enterprise, it appears.'

'Dash on, will you?' she replied.

With Becky's words of insistence in our ears, Mr Furst and I were quickly out the door searching for a cab. Fortunately, one was just pulling around the corner as we stepped to the curb, and I waved it down. 'Waterloo Station, driver, with haste, if you please.'

Several long minutes later, our hansom pulled up at the main entrance of the London terminal. Unfortunately, our desire for a speedy trip had been met with heavy carriage and foot traffic around the streets leading to the station.

I paid the driver, who was not pleased with having to change a one-pound note. Quickly, Mr Furst and I hurried into the crowded terminal.

'I'll secure a train schedule and find out when the next train for Andover will be leaving,' I said.

'I will be right behind you,' Mr Furst replied.

Checking the schedule and seeing that the next train to Andover would leave in just a little more than fifteen minutes, I shouted, 'We're in luck, Mr Furst! We've only a few minutes to wait.' Turning, I could see that Mr Furst was nowhere in sight. 'Dash it all! Where could the man have gone?'

I knew he could not have gotten far, but I also suspected he could take care of himself if needs called for it. I bought two first-class carriage tickets and scanned the crowd for Mr Furst. Finally, I spotted him speaking with a uniformed Metropolitan police officer near the newsstand.

'Ah, there you are, Mr Furst. I thought you'd gotten lost amongst the masses or worse. Our train leaves in a few minutes from platform seven,' I said as I checked my watch. For a moment, I remembered my colonel presenting the gold timepiece to me upon my retirement from the Rifles. What a bittersweet day that was! And then, just as quickly, I was again back in the moment.

'I was speaking with Constable Henderson, here, about the police headquarters in Andover. He told me all the main police stations are now linked by telephone. Is that not amazing, Mr Mayne?'

'Yes, yes, quite amazin', Mr Furst,' I said anxiously. 'We really must get a move on if we're to make the Andover train. Follow on quickly now, Mr Furst.' It was as if I had a child in tow. Although I was confident he was quite familiar with American rail travel, Mr Furst seemed amazed at the British train system. We found platform seven without trouble and our first-class carriage. For some reason, Mr Furst was surprised that entrance to the compartment was gained from outside the train.

'What? You mean we do not need first to board the train where the cars couple and then find our compartment from within?' he asked.

'No,' I answered as I swung open the carriage compartment door and led Mr Furst to where our seats were waiting.

'We might as well get comfortable,' I said. 'Our trip will take one hour and thirty minutes before we arrive at Andover Station. Would you care for a nectar drop?' I offered the candy from the small brown paper bag I carried in my overcoat. 'They're my favourite sweet.'

Mr Furst enthusiastically accepted my offer of the hard candy and tossed the small ruby-red piece into his mouth with aplomb. I watched in amazed curiosity as he quickly swept the sweet from one side of his mouth to the other and back again—his tongue, continually in motion. As hard as he might have tried to keep his composure, his watering blue eyes betrayed his obvious discomfort. Stealthily, he reached for his handkerchief and, placing it to his mouth, ejected the drop into it.

'Whew! That is some piece of spicy candy,' he said.

'Yes, but it's an acquired taste, sir. Not for everyone, you know? I believe they're red-hot cinnamon drops,' I said, suppressing a smile.

With a sharp jerk of the carriages and an intermittent chirping of the steel wheels, the train slowly pulled out of the station. We were on our way.

Chapter 12
The Train Ride to Andover and Our Grizzly Discovery

As we were beyond the city's sights, Mr Furst appeared mesmerised by the blur of the scenic countryside rushing by his window. In the silence, boredom quickly overtook me, and I looked about the compartment for something to read, anything that a previous traveller might have discarded or forgotten. To my amazement, peeking out from under the compartment seat on Mr Furst's side, I could see the corner of a periodical and the remains of an old *Times*. Interested in anything to help while away the time, I got down on hands and knees to retrieve one or the other. I pulled out the periodical, leaving the *Times* perhaps for later. As luck would have it, my find was a not-too-old copy of *The Union Jack*.

Mr Furst observed my actions, of course. 'What on earth are you doing down on the floor, Mr Mayne, and what have you there?'

'What, this? Why, it's just a discarded copy o' a weekly penny story paper,' I said. 'I thought I might have a read since I didn't wish to disturb you and your thoughts. We do have quite some time before we arrive in Andover.'

'Actually, Mr Mayne, I would welcome this opportunity to speak with you on a subject that has absolutely nothing to do with the case. I was just now thinking of how best to broach the subject with you.'

I didn't know what to think or how to respond. Mr Furst was so unpredictable. 'Oh, yes?'

'Since I have related to you my family history, all the facts surrounding this case, and why I have gotten so entangled in it, I thought that you might wish to share one or two vignettes of your campaign exploits, soldier to soldier, so to speak. What do you say? Truth be told, you know more about me than I, you. Further, if we are to be partners in future inquiry work, I believe that I should know much more about you and your experiences. Would you not agree?'

Mr Furst had indeed caught me off guard with his request. I did rather want to share *some* of my many adventures with him. He had started to give me a view into his life with his colourful vignettes. Understand, reader, I wanted to be as forthcoming, but there were parts of my life, especially the end of my military career and what may have caused me to leave the queen's service, which I believed were much too private, too personal for me to share. I hadn't known Mr Furst all that long. In fact, although I was learning more about him, I barely knew the man at all. To bare my soul to him was an act I wasn't at ease doing, at least not at that time. I lay *The Union Jack* next to me and looked into Furst's waiting eyes. 'What would you like to know, Mr Furst?'

'I would like to know as much about your life as you feel comfortable telling, especially about such a long career spent in service to your queen and country. I must tell you that your sister has made me understand that you were awarded the Victoria Cross for some act of uncommon valour in South Africa during the recent war with the Dutch settlers, the Boers. I am aware that the queen does not award that medal willy-nilly. You may not be aware, Mr Mayne, that the Victoria Cross is equivalent to my country's Medal of Honor, the highest military award given for acts of heroism above and beyond the call of duty. Furthermore, the President of the United States presents it to its distinguished recipients. I believe your award was most likely presented to you by your queen. Am I not correct?'

It was true that I was proud of the honour that my queen had bestowed upon me with the medal, but I wasn't proud of the circumstances under which she had awarded it to me. Yes, the queen awarded the medal to me, but it seemed, at least to me, that I had ordered Tommy to his death to gain it! To me, his loss was not worth the prize. No, I wasn't prepared to talk about the details of this part of my life with Mr Furst, a relative stranger, or with anyone closer.

'Yes, you are correct, Mr Furst. The queen did pin the medal on me, and it was a great honour, but it was simply for doin' my duty as the Army had trained me to do it—nothing more. There is nothing else about it what I would care to tell. It's all quite private and personal, don't you see, Mr Furst?'

'Yes, I do see. I also perceive, however, Mr Mayne, that there is much more to the story than that. Please understand, Mr Mayne, that if or when you are ready to talk about it, I am here to listen with an empathetic ear. Regardless, if you are uncomfortable telling it to me, so be it.'

'Thank you, sir, for your understanding and for not pressin' me for more. The last battle o' the late war was a terrible experience for me—an experience what I don't care to revisit.'

'Mr Mayne, I fear that you and I have seen many things in combat that most likely we would prefer to be able to forget. In my country, the phrase is "seeing the elephant." A quaint expression, no? As an officer, my duty often forced me to send men into battle to accomplish missions I feared would lead to their deaths. Unfortunately, I was correct in my predictions many times. We have to live with that knowledge, but it need not cripple our souls, Mr Mayne,' Mr Furst said, most compassionately.

Afterwards, he turned again toward the window, his voice trailing off with his last words. I picked up *The Union Jack* and tried to read, but Mr Furst's comments on war echoed in my ears, and images of Tommy lying dead at my feet filled my head. I could feel my eyes beginning to tear up, so I held the story paper to screen my face, hoping that the perceptive Mr Furst would not catch on.

Shortly, the conductor was in the corridor outside our compartment, demanding our tickets to Andover. I slid the door open and handed them to the man, who punched them and returned them to me. 'Big fire in Andover last night, I heard,' the conductor said. 'Couple blokes died in it. Hope they wasn't mates o' yours,' he added, apparently noticing my tear-streaked cheek as he slid the compartment door closed.

If Mr Furst noticed my face during the conductor's brief visit, he didn't say so. He continued looking out the window, and I read. Nothing more passed between Mr Furst and me until the conductor called out, 'Andover! Andover station!' as he made his way through the corridor.

'Well, now. Here already,' Mr Furst stated in a sarcastic voice as he checked his watch, making light, no doubt, as to the long ride. I checked my watch, as well. It was nearly past four. As expected, the train had arrived on schedule.

We detrained. After getting directions from a railway employee, we were off on foot for the Andover police station. It was only a block or two to the relatively small granite building that was home to the local constabulary. Once there, we inquired whether Mr Sherlock Holmes had informed them that we would arrive.

'Mr Sherlock 'Olmes, you say?' quizzed the duty sergeant. 'I've 'eard o' 'im, o' course, Gov. Who 'asn't? But he 'asn't been 'ere…at least not in recent mem'ry. Should 'e be 'ere, sir?' The sergeant turned to the inspector, just coming out of his office, who confirmed that Sherlock Holmes had not been at Andover, at least not to the station.

Mr Furst introduced us and explained the note we had received without going into great detail. The Andover inspector's name was Haney.

'Mr Charles Underwood, you say?' Inspector Haney asked, glancing at the sergeant. 'Strange that you should ask for him. The bodies of him and another man were discovered burnt to death at Mr Underwood's Cross Lane residence early this morning.'

'I'm sorry, but are you quite certain, Inspector Haney,' Mr Furst asked, 'that it was Underwood?'

'Quite certain, Mr Furst. The remains of Charles Underwood were positively identified by his housekeeper from his queer-shaped right foot. It's a bloody shame to lose such a national celebrity as Mr Underwood. An American, you probably would not know that he was renowned in English theatre as "The Man of Ten-Thousand Faces." Why, he could create entirely new identities with but a wig and a bit of stage makeup. A terrible loss, indeed.'

'What of the other man, Inspector? Has he been identified?' Mr Furst asked.

'From what we could tell, he was a short little fellow, and his clothing had a French cut to it. His body was horribly burned—and other than an odd-shaped piece of melted metal, he had nothing on his body to identify him,' the Inspector said.

'If it would not be too much trouble,' said Mr Furst, 'may I see the metal, Inspector?'

'This is quite irregular, Mr Furst. Do you think that you might know the man?'

'Quite possibly. May I see it, please?'

'Well, since you are an acquaintance of Mr Sherlock Holmes, I should think your examination of the piece would be all right. It was found, of all places, inside the cuff of the deceased's boot.'

Inspector Haney produced a somewhat melted gold-toned piece of metal from a wooden file cabinet at the back of the room. 'Here it is,' he said.

Mr Furst took the piece, turning it over in his hand again and again. 'Have you a magnifying glass, Inspector?' Taking the glass from the Inspector, Mr Furst re-examined the piece. His eyes suddenly grew large, and his mouth fell agape. 'Oh, my! What have we here? I can barely read a few small, slightly distorted letters, *u-r-g*, and here, *i-v-e*,' exclaimed Mr Furst.

'Does that mean anything to you, Mr Furst?' asked the Inspector.

'Inspector, I believe that this melted hunk of metal was once the badge belonging to William Mason, a former city detective with the Harrisburg, Pennsylvania Police Bureau, and one of two men I am seeking for murder, theft, and arson back home. I believe that it is by pure luck and our good fortune that this item survived the fire. Also, I am certain that the second man, Simon McCreedy, never suspected that Mason would have any trace of identification on his person that could link him to McCreedy and his sinister plans. Do you know how the fire started—accident or intentional?'

'All appearances give one the impression that the two men had been drinking and smoking late at night. Mr Underwood had been known to be quite the drinker. Perhaps they passed out, and their cigars may have set loose writing papers on fire,' Inspector Haney said.

'It is a strange thing, though. The housekeeper discovered the bodies of both men near the study's locked door. Oddly, it appears that someone unknown might have locked the door from the outside,' the Inspector continued. 'The housekeeper, who had not been in the house since the morning before, could not explain why the study door might have become locked. It could not have locked on its own. We suspect foul play. However, we have no clues as to who might have been the person or persons responsible for the deaths.'

'My educated guess is that it was Simon McCreedy who locked the door after setting fire to block the victims' exit,' said Mr Furst, 'to cover up his having been there and his part in the fatal conflagration. Undoubtedly, he is tying up loose ends before making his run for The Royal Small Arms Factory at Enfield. Mr Mayne, the note your sister received from the unknown man must have been delivered by McCreedy, himself, in disguise, most probably provided by the late Mr Underwood. His plan, no doubt, was to deliver the note luring us out of the city and away from Enfield.

'McCreedy has played me the fool!' said Mr Furst, a tone of disappointment mixed with disgust to his voice. 'Further, it is apparent that McCreedy sent us here on a wild goose chase to keep us away so that he would have a clear path to Mr Rigby. Furthermore, most likely, you and I have been observed by either Mason or McCreedy from the very beginning. Your sister may have even noticed McCreedy at the Lion's Claw when we had lunch there. Perhaps something about his bearing or his posture seemed familiar to her. Regardless, we must contact Inspector Lestrade at once!

'Inspector Haney, if you have a telephone instrument here at the station, would you please try to contact Chief Inspector G. Lestrade of Scotland Yard immediately? It is a matter of national and, quite possibly, international security. We cannot let the murderous fiend,

McCreedy, slip away, for I fear if we do, we shall never retrieve the plans and put an end to the villain's cunning but diabolical run.'

97

CHAPTER 13
IT IS TO BIRMINGHAM WE SHALL GO

'Mr Furst, it is my opinion that the telephone apparatus is a piece of foolish extravagance,' Inspector Haney said. 'Regardless, headquarters required we have one installed. That was a little over one month ago. We have never needed to use it, though. Fortunately, however, I have received instructions for its operation. If you think there is a need to bother Scotland Yard, well then, I suppose I will have to make use of the blasted thing.'

'I assure you, Inspector, it is most important to contact the Chief Inspector there. He is aware of the details of the case and has offered assistance where and when needed,' Furst replied.

After several unsuccessful attempts, Inspector Haney finally communicated through the apparatus to a constable, presumably at Scotland Yard. Haney related the communication to us: *No, Chief Inspector Lestrade was not available, but if Inspector Haney would leave a message, the constable would inform Lestrade of the desire that he should return his call just as soon as he should arrive from whence he presently was.* Once Haney had given us the particulars of the message, he returned the piece of the apparatus he'd been holding to his ear into its carriage with a sharp 'clack.'

'Blasted piece of uselessness!' Haney huffed.

'Inspector Haney,' Mr Furst said. 'If I might, it appears the telephone equipment worked reasonably well, given the circumstances. I am quite certain Chief Inspector Lestrade will return your communication once he becomes aware of who was calling and about what you called.'

It was more than an hour before a jangling sound from a box near the telephone apparatus brought me back from my thoughts. I checked my gold watch. It was nearly half six.

'Yes, this is Inspector Haney,' he said into the apparatus mouthpiece. 'Mr Siderus Furst? Right here.'

'Here, Mr Furst,' Haney said as he handed over the mouth and earpieces. 'It is an Inspector Gregson of Scotland Yard.'

Mr Furst put the earpiece to his head and spoke into the mouthpiece. 'This is Furst.' He repeated what was relayed to him so that we all might know. 'When Inspector Lestrade received our message, he contacted Superintendent Rigby at Enfield? Please speak up, Inspector. Thank you. He said no one had contacted him regarding plans or meetings to discuss guns of any kind? That is strange. Thank you for the information, Inspector Gregson. Oh, and pass along my gratitude to Chief Inspector Lestrade for his cooperation, as well. Yes, thank you. Goodbye.'

Mr Furst appeared dumbfounded as he returned the earpiece to its cradle. He stared at the floor in silence while pacing back and forth, and I thought it best not to disturb him from his thoughts. After a few moments, he stopped and turned to me sharply.

'Do you still possess your Army service pistol?' Mr Furst asked.

'Why, yes, I was allowed to keep it upon my retirement. I have it with me now,' I said. 'I brought it along in the off chance that I might need it. Why do you ask?'

'Who is the manufacturer of your handgun?' Mr Furst asked.

'Why, it's a trusty Webley revolver. Why do you ask, Mr Furst?'

'Yes, of course! I now believe that McCreedy, somehow knowing we had already made Superintendent Rigby aware of a possible meeting, has undoubtedly changed his target to the Webley and Son Firearms Company. That would be my second choice if I were him. If I am not mistaken, and this time I believe that I am not, the Webley Company is located in Birmingham. Is that far from here?' Mr Furst asked.

It is more than a three-hour ride from Andover by train,' said Haney. 'I am unsure, however, if there are any Birmingham-bound trains due through here very soon.'

Upon hearing that, I retrieved from my coat pocket the train schedule I had taken at Waterloo Station and checked it to verify what Haney had offered. 'We're in luck,' I said. There *is* a train to Birmingham what leaves from Andover Station at 7:45, and it arrives in Birmingham New Street Station at 11:17.'

'Well, it shall be a long night,' said Mr Furst. 'We should make arrangements to be on that train and try to get some sleep during the trip. Bright and early tomorrow morning, we must be at Webley and Son. We shall then see what damage has been done to our plans due to my inexcusable lapse in deductive skills.'

We thanked Inspector Haney for his kindness, professional courtesy, and cooperation and bade him and his desk sergeant a good evening. Mr Furst stared at the ground silently on our walk to the train station. Each step he took appeared to be laboured and plodding. He was, most likely, disappointed in himself for falling for McCreedy's ruse, which sent us in this very wrong direction. Still, to my mind, it was also apparent he had uncovered some most valuable intelligence. McCreedy was now without his accomplice, Mason.

Further, I believed Mr Furst would discover McCreedy no matter what disguise he now wore. Trusting there were no words I could use to console my companion, I chose to keep silent until such time when he was ready to converse. After purchasing our tickets for Birmingham, I joined Mr Furst on the bench, where he waited for our train. I noticed he was gently massaging the part of his leg above its artificial component. Still, he said nothing.

To perhaps take his mind off of thoughts of failure or to distract him from his leg, I spoke. 'Inspector Haney is undoubtedly a fine cove—so helpful and accommodatin'. Wouldn't you agree, Mr Furst?'

'Hmm? What is that—a "cove," you say? What in the world is that, Mr Mayne?'

'"Cove" is slang for chap or fellow, don't you see?'

'Yes, I do see. I have so much to learn about England. I am happy to have such a terrific guide as you and such a friend to try to help take my mind off my troubles,' Mr Furst said, a smile broadening into a grin.

He had seen through my ploy and called me "friend." I had not expected that.

At 7:30, by my watch, our train pulled into Andover Station. I led the way to our carriage, opened the door, and stepped inside. Mr Furst slowly followed. At precisely 7:45, the train pulled away from the station. We were fortunate once again to have an empty compartment and the use of all its seats to ourselves. There were few passengers at that hour, and I was convinced that Mr Furst and I were not destined to share the compartment with other travellers that night.

As during the previous train ride, Mr Furst stared out of the window. Only now, there was nothing to see through the window glass into the darkness except for the image of a solemn viewer reflecting back on himself. I wondered if he was reflecting upon more than just his image. However, I let him keep to his thoughts without interruption.

The compartment was void of reading materials, so I settled back into my seat and closed my eyes. The gentle rocking motion of the carriage and the monotonous clickity-click of steel wheels over the small gaps between the rails soon put me to sleep. I remained asleep until the conductor rapped on the door, demanding our tickets. I lazily handed them to him, and upon the conclusion of the transaction, I continued my slumber. As I slipped into a deep sleep, a dream, more the nightmare I had often experienced in recent nights, fought its way to the fore, past whatever pleasant reveries might be in more peace-filled times. Once again, I was in the high African grasses that flowed like a lush green ocean around Majuba Hill and surrounded by the finest young soldiers that Britain had produced. Though unsure why our officers had chosen this piece of ground to defend, we didn't question their orders. That day, the regiment would plainly "do and die" in still one more battle of the Boer War, the war that would prove to be a significant military disaster and an embarrassment to the British Empire.

With so many of our regimental senior and junior officers killed, wounded, or taken prisoner, the command devolved to the noncommissioned ranks. As I was the senior regimental sergeant, the responsibility of the leadership rested with me. Observing our brave lads' slaughter on the adjacent hill, I ordered as many riflemen as I could safely spare to give relief and join the outnumbered defenders there. Corporal Tommy Atkins, my friend since boyhood and husband to my dear Becky, was among those I sent. I had first commanded the main body of riflemen to cover the retreat of all those who could withdraw from the hill where I had sent Tommy and Number One

Company. I ordered continuous fire on the Boer sharpshooters, many of whom were mere boys with rifles, until the evacuation could be completed.

After the battle was over and the Boers allowed us to recover our dead and the wounded who were too bad off to be taken prisoner, I found the bullet-torn body of Tommy. Because of the terrible head and face wounds he had received, he was barely recognizable. I attempted to pick up his blood-drenched body in my arms, but my strength failed. I called to a young Highlander, but when he saw the terrible condition of Tommy's body, he became physically ill. Fortunately, an older rifleman came to my aid, and we carried Tommy to a shady spot behind a pile of rocks. I saluted my brave friend, turned, and rejoined my regiment.

Because of my actions, the generals said, I had saved most of the regiment and kept our colours. For those reasons, the queen awarded me the Cross. Tommy got his cross, too, a wooden one near the spot where I had laid him. Oh, many praised me for my cool-headedness under fire and the decisive actions I had taken. The Army even offered me the opportunity to return to England and Sandhurst to attend officers' school. Still, I was no "gentleman." I knew that would never do. I was finished— I could no longer "soldier on." Tommy and I would fight no more together.

The irony of it all was that the Battle of Majuba Hill was the last battle of the Boer War. I was going home, back to England, and Becky. How was I to face her, knowing that I had sent our Tommy to his death? The monotonous rocking of the troopship and some Jamaican rum I "borrowed" from one of the Navy lads helped keep me numb— the constant rocking, the constant rocking, the rocking—

'Mr Mayne, Mr Mayne, wake up! We are arriving.' The face of Furst appeared inches from my own. His firm but gentle hand was upon my shoulder, rocking me, pulling me back from my restless slumber. 'I would ask if you had a pleasant sleep, but I know it was anything but.'

'Oh, how so?' I asked.

'Well, for one thing, you were tossing violently. At one point, I feared you might pitch yourself from your seat. For another, you were shouting commands as if you were directing a battle. Wherever you were in your nightmare, I know it must have been hell on earth, my good man.'

'Did I say anything, anything at all, what was intelligible in my delirium, Mr Furst?'

'You said enough for me to freely admit you have nothing more to say to me about that which you have apparently long been keeping locked up inside. Please know I understand and will no longer hound you about your wartime experiences.'

'Thank you kindly, Mr Furst. You are *truly* an empathetic gentleman.'

'Not at all, my friend, not at all,' he said as we detrained. 'Shall we grab a bit of sustenance wherever we may be able to find it at this late hour, make our plan, and then reconnoitre the Webley and Son's establishment?'

'We shall, Mr Furst. We shall.'

As we walked down the platform to the turnstile that led to the exit from the train station, I stopped a busy conductor walking in the opposite direction. 'Pardon me, but can you tell us where we might find food and beverage within a short walk?'

'Sorry mate, can't help ye. I'm not from 'ere,' he said. 'But you might inquire o' that constable what is standing near the "out door" just beyond the turnstile.' And then he hurried on his way toward the trains.

'Before we go any farther, Mr Mayne,' Mr Furst said, stopping and tugging my coat sleeve. 'If you agree and can find a telegraph office, I suggest you send a telegram to Becky, *er*, Mrs Atkins, apprising her of where we now are. If she is not worried, I am almost certain she is curious about why we have not returned to London. I suppose she will not receive it tonight. However, she should have it bright and early tomorrow morning. What do you say, Mr Mayne?'

It caught me off-guard that Mr Furst referred to my sister as "Becky," even if it might have been a slip of his tongue. Mind you, I didn't, in clear conscience, care that he used the "familiar" concerning my sister. However, I was surprised nonetheless.

'Why, yes, Mr Furst. You are correct. I should send a telegraph to her, and I'll do that immediately. There is always a telegraph office to be found at train stations.'

I found the office near the exit door of the station. As cheaply as I could manage, I sent *Becky dear, we are safe in Birmingham. Will be home tomorrow. Baddy*. Although hungry and tired, I felt content and self-satisfied for sending the telegram. I returned to the spot where I had left Mr Furst only moments before. But instead of him being there, I spotted him talking with the constable on the sidewalk outside the station. I hurried to join the two men just as Mr Furst was concluding his conversation.

'What now, Mr Furst? Are we off to find food and drink?' I panted as I reached for my handkerchief to wipe my brow.

'Not quite yet, my friend. I believe it prudent that we first visit the Birmingham Police Station and see if we might apprise Scotland Yard of our change of plan. Do you not think that is a wise move? I understand the station is located in Steel House Lane, which may be a bit far for us to "hoof it." Have you adequate funds for a couple more carriage rides, or should we start walking?'

I checked my left coat pocket for the balance of the money Becky had loaned us. 'I believe we might have enough to cover that and somewhat more. However, we may not have enough money to get us back to London.'

'Do not fear, Mr Mayne, I am confident that banks here in Birmingham will honour my cheque. If not, we may stay in Birmingham for a while, eh? I am certain this is a wonderful city.'

I felt my gold watch in my pocket and decided that, if needed, I would pawn it to cover our expenses until I received additional funds from Mr Furst. Either way, I was committed to seeing this case through to the end with Mr Furst.

CHAPTER 14
BIRMINGHAM -- THE CONFRONTATION AWAITS

Exhausted from the restless slumber on the train, I didn't answer Mr Furst. Instead, like a puppy dog, I followed him outside the station to the curb where we might find cabs standing. Sure enough, Mr Furst's luck was holding. There, with its driver dozing on top, was a lone hansom.

'Hoy, there, driver!' Mr Furst shouted. 'Police headquarters on Steel House Lane, if you please.'

'Gi' on in, then, gov,' the driver said. ''Tis a bit late for a trip to the coppers, ain't it?'

'Never mind that!' I snapped as we boarded the cab.

'No need to nause!' the cabbie snapped back.

Even though it was several blocks to the police station, we rode in silence. The only sounds were the horse's hoofs as they struck the Birmingham street cobblestones and the occasional crack of the driver's whip as it snapped the night air.

Several minutes later, the cab pulled to a jolting stop in front of a dingy-looking red brick building with a constable standing guard at the top of its marble steps. Mr Furst and I de-cabbed, and I paid the driver the exact fare, which caused the man to grimace and stick his tongue out at me. 'Bugger off!' he mumbled as he drove off into the night.

Unfazed, I led Mr Furst up the steps to where the constable stood post.

'State your business, or be on yer way with ye,' the uniformed gatekeeper said sternly.

'We desire to speak with your inspector on duty. We must get a message to Scotland Yard as quickly as possible. It is a matter most imperative,' Mr Furst said.

'Imperative, ye say? I guess we'll see about that! Wait 'ere,' the constable said as he entered the building, slamming its heavy wooden door firmly behind him.

Moments later, the constable reappeared and beckoned us to enter the station. 'Well, come on in quick, will ye. I'm no a bloody doorman,' the grumpy policeman grunted.

A dapper-looking gentleman met us in impeccable attire just inside the door. His raven hair was slick and parted in the middle, even at this late hour, and his matching moustache was trimmed and waxed.

'I am Inspector Morris. What may I do to assist you, gentlemen, at this late hour?' he asked. 'I understand that you want to send a message of some importance to my colleagues in London. Is that correct?'

Mr Furst nodded, introduced us, and began his story, one which he'd shared several times since he'd started his quest. Additionally, he mentioned his association with Chief Inspector Lestrade, meeting with Inspector Haney in Andover, and speaking via telephone to Inspector Gregson in London earlier in the evening. Further, Mr Furst told of his certainty that a meeting between Superintendent Philip Webley of Webley and Son and the murderer, arsonist, and thief, Simon McCreedy, would most surely occur the following morning at the

Webley factory. He told of his belief that another terrible hoax was about to be perpetrated yet one more time—this time on English soil.

'I see,' said Morris. 'Please pardon me, Mr Furst, for being sceptical, but I do not know either of you two gentlemen, and I have nothing but your theory of something terrible that *may* happen in the morning at Webley's. You do see my predicament, do you not?'

'Yes, of course, I do understand, Inspector. However, if you will kindly telephone Scotland Yard, the inspectors there will vouch for us.' Mr Furst pleaded.

'I am very sorry, but our telephone has been unusable for the past four days,' Morris said. 'So, even if I wanted to contact Scotland Yard, I could not. Further, I will not expend precious police resources to accompany you to Webley's on what may very well be a chase of some phantom wild goose. Mr Webley is a very important and generous man, employing vast numbers of skilled people from our city. I will not be the one to embarrass him in front of them, especially in his own factory. I am afraid you are on your own on that account. However, mind you, if you cause trouble for Mr Webley, rest assured I shall arrest you both. So, do tread carefully, gentlemen, if you please.'

'Very well, Inspector, if that is how the matter must be left,' said Mr Furst. 'One more thing though, before we leave, if you do not mind. Would you be kind enough to point us in the direction of the Webley factory and tell us if there might be a public house open at this hour?'

'The Webley factory is situated in Weaman Street if you are still intent on going there,' Morris shared. 'Turn right at the end of this street and walk five or six blocks. At that point, you will see Weaman Street on your left, and you will find the lengthy Webley factory buildings along there. Regarding pubs, you might try the Sir John

Falstaff, but I doubt it will be open at this hour. It, too, is in Weaman Street.'

'Thank you, Inspector Morris. I am grateful for whatever assistance you could give us,' Mr Furst said, bowing slightly. 'If your telephone becomes operational once again, please get in touch with Chief Inspector G. Lestrade of Scotland Yard and advise him that we have spoken. I am confident we shall meet again, Inspector. Good night.'

Mr Furst was already heading for the door, and I had to rush to keep up with the man who now appeared intent to begin the late-night walk to Weaman Street. He did not seem fatigued in the slightest from our train ride and meeting with Inspector Morris. Indeed, strangely, he appeared invigorated. Perhaps it was the anticipation of the hoped-for confrontation with McCreedy and the recovery of the plans and second prototype pistol that drove him so.

'Keep up, will you, Mr Mayne. If a cripple like me can do it, a seasoned soldier like you can, as well. We have only a few more blocks of walking before we reach Weaman Street.'

I picked up the pace and matched each of Mr Furst's steps with one of my own. The clicking of Mr Furst's artificial leg set a cadence to which I marched. Before long, we reached the corner where Weaman Street began. In the distance, we could see the long brick factory buildings of Webley and Son Firearms. A block or two more brought us to the entrance which proclaimed *Company Office*.

'Right! We are at Number 81 Weaman,' Mr Furst announced. 'This is the entrance we shall use tomorrow morning. Now, let us find the pub that Inspector Morris mentioned. What was the name?'

'I believe it's called the Sir John Falstaff, what he suggested, and there it is nearly directly across the street from this very entrance,' I said, feeling relieved that our walking was at an end for the evening. 'It looks to be closed up for the night, but I see a faint light comin' from one o' the unshuttered windows. Perhaps your luck will continue to hold, Mr Furst, and we may find a place to rest our weary bones until the morning.'

We crossed the deserted street to the pub. I tried the door, but it was locked. I pounded on it with my fist three times. Finally, after a minute or so, a white-haired gent, whom I took to be the proprietor, opened the door just a crack.

'Wot is it? Can't ye see wir closed? Go away and don't come back 'til midday tomorrow,' he said.

'Show him some money, Mr Mayne. Perhaps you can entice him to allow us admittance if nothing more than sit in warmth and peace,' said Mr Furst.

'Two pounds for your trouble, sir, if you'll just let us in to sit until morning. We ask for no food or drink—only to sit and be warm,' I pleaded.

'Two pounds, ye say? You won'ts make no trouble, will ye?' the man asked, stroking his stubbly chin whiskers.

'Not at all, my good man. Do we have a bargain?' I asked.

'Not s'posed to do this, but you looks to be gemmen. Hurry, come on in wit ye,' the man whispered as he snatched the two one-pound notes from my fingers. 'The fire is out for the night, but for another quid, I could light it up for ye. What say ye?'

I looked at Mr Furst. 'That is a dear price what to pay for a little warmth, Mr Furst.'

'If you have the funds, pay the man, Mr Mayne. We will not be able to afford to return to London until I can get to a bank, anyway.'

'As you wish, Mr Furst,' I said. 'Here you are, my good man. Here's your pound. We'll need to remain here until Webley's opens in the mornin', so build a nice warm fire, if you don't mind.'

'As ye wish, gemmen, as ye wish,' the man said. 'I'll unlatch the door when I gets up.' With that, the old proprietor built a roaring fire and slipped up the stairs to his bed, no doubt feeling three pounds richer for his little trouble.

We had nothing to do and hours before we could visit the Webley factory. Mr Furst suggested we play a few hands of Brag after he spied a deck of playing cards on a nearby table. Since Mr Furst held no coins of his own, and I held the total of our bank in my coat pocket, we decided to play for points instead. We played on into the wee hours. Mr Furst must have been tired, as he was definitely behind in points. We grew bored with the game and were too tired to continue any further conversation.

Soon, the warmth of the fire and the sight of a couple of not-too-uncomfortable-looking benches found us coiling up as best we could, hoping for a few hours of sleep before whatever unknown encounter might find us later in the morning. Mr Furst unstrapped and set aside his artificial leg, and soon he was asleep. I was amazed that with the chase finally coming to an end and with what possibly might become a violent confrontation in the morning at Webley's, Mr Furst could sleep so soundly. Mine, however, was a restless slumber. I was concerned about how Mr Furst might react upon seeing his father's murderer. What would he do? What would McCreedy do, and what part might I play in the meeting, if anything at all? These questions weighed heavily on my mind as I finally drifted off into what I might call a half-sleep. It was the same as when I was in Africa, awaiting the next day's action. It was, I suppose, the anticipation of the unknown. Whatever it was to be, I would be unswerving in my devotion to the cause, through thick or thin, with Mr Furst, be it for better or worse.

Chapter 15

The Next Morning – The Confrontation at Webley's

Tuesday morning, September 19, around five o'clock, found Mr Siderus Furst and me far from our homes, hungry and waking to the stirrings of the proprietor of the Sir John Falstaff pub. He was busy tidying up the establishment as he made his way toward us. The two of us sat up as straight as we could, stiff and achy for having slept as babes curled in our mothers' wombs for hours. Mr Furst quickly reattached his leg as the man approached.

'Cor blimey!' the proprietor exclaimed at having witnessed Mr Furst's act of reattaching his artificial limb. Then, without further mention of what he had seen, he said, 'You gemmen have a good night's sleep, did ye? I should charge ye the lodgin' ye knows?'

'Yes, I agree. You should be paid something extra for your trouble,' Mr Furst said, looking questioningly at me. 'We might be willing to pay you for that and, perhaps, some coffee or tea. Could that be arranged?'

'Blimey!' the old man exclaimed. 'Next, you'll be wantin' bloomin' bangers and mash. Well, I do have the coffee on, and yer welcome to it, that is, fer a mere shillin' apiece. That is, if you blokes can spare it?'

I nodded, confirming Mr Furst's belief in the balance of our rapidly diminishing funds.

'I believe we've got that much, and perhaps a little more for you if we can drink our coffee near one o' the street windows, that is, once you've unshuttered them,' I said. 'We need to see the comings and goings at Webley's when they open, and then we'll happily leave you richer than when you first met us.'

The proprietor winked, bowed slightly, and went into the kitchen area, presumably to get our coffees.

'Well played, Mr Mayne," Mr Furst said as he shuffled over to a table nearer a window at the front of the pub overlooking Weaman Street. 'From this vantage point, we should be able to see when Philip Webley and Simon McCreedy arrive for their meeting. I will assume that as the owner, Mr Webley will arrive early. Anyone's guess is when McCreedy might arrive. When he does arrive, I suspect he will be in the disguise that the late Mr Underwood created for him.'

'Quite so,' I said. 'If McCreedy's as disfigured as what you say, he'd want to draw as little attention to himself as possible. Will you recognise him from here when he arrives, Mr Furst?'

'His form is burnt into my brain and soul, Mr Mayne. I shall recognise him, disguised or not.'

A few minutes later, the proprietor brought our coffees, and I paid him the agreed-upon two shillings plus an additional shiny sovereign for his trouble.

'Thank ye kindly, sirs,' the proprietor said, bowing stiffly. 'We don't get gemman of yer cut here so much. I'll unlock the door, open the shutters, and ye can stay as long as ye needs and leave when ye wants. Thank ye kindly.'

We thanked the man for his hospitality and continued drinking our coffees as we peered out the now-unshuttered window overlooking Weaman Street and the factory beyond.

At precisely six o'clock, a shiny Clarence, drawn by a beautiful white mare, pulled smartly up to the office entrance of Webley's and discharged its lone passenger. As the coach departed, we could see an imposing-looking older man with a full grey beard, impressively dressed in the latest English gentleman's attire, carrying himself with an air of importance. The man held a small leather portmanteau in his right hand by its handle, and it must have been burdensome as the man leaned in its direction as he walked. As he reached the door, he was greeted by what one might term the factory's security officer. The uniformed officer opened the door for the older man and closely followed him into the building.

'From his dress and bearing, Mr Mayne, I surmise that gentleman can be none other than Mr Philip Webley,' Mr Furst stated as a slight smile broadened. 'The cheese is in the trap, Mr Mayne. Now, for the rat. You may be wondering why we do not attempt to meet with Webley before McCreedy arrives, my friend.'

'Well, now that you mention it, why yes, it did cross my mind, sir.'

'McCreedy could arrive at any moment. If he saw me, he would run, and we would need to chase him elsewhere and perhaps lose him. In fact, he could be watching the factory at this very moment, ensuring that it is safe for him to enter. Also, on the off-chance that I am wrong, and there is no meeting, we run the risk of running afoul of Inspector Morris.'

I nodded my understanding of our predicament, saying nothing. I merely kept watching with Mr Furst, hoping that McCreedy would show up sooner than later. To be completely honest, reader, my nerves were on edge, and I had an uncomfortable, nauseating feeling in the pit of my stomach. I had experienced the same feeling before every battle I had fought in my long military career. It was a feeling that I never truly shook. Old soldiers might try to tell you they feared nothing, but they were only fooling themselves.

Near seven o'clock, a tired-looking constable and our recent acquaintance, Inspector Morris, entered the pub. I presumed they were coming off their night duty tour and were there for a cup of coffee, or a bit more, before going home. Mr Furst, intent on viewing the Webley office building, didn't notice the two law enforcement officers. Unfortunately, we did not pass unnoticed by the Inspector, who came over to our table.

'Ah, the Londoner and the American are still here. Keeping watch for your diabolical phantom, are you?'

Mr Furst did not look in the Inspector's direction but spoke somewhat rudely. 'Ah, good morning, Inspector Morris. I see you have a keen grasp of the obvious. As we are bothering no one, I am hopeful you will allow us to enjoy our coffee in peace without undue aggravation. We would ask you to join us, but we will not be staying long.' Mr Furst suddenly became silent, ghostly so, and his eyes widened. 'In fact, Inspector, Mr Mayne and I must leave immediately. Come, Mr Mayne, we must bid farewell to the Inspector and conclude our business.'

'Mind you, Mr Furst, cause no trouble in my city!' the Inspector warned. 'Our jails are not for gentlemen.'

'Thank you for your concern for our comfort, Inspector,' Mr Furst said as he rose and briskly walked to the door. 'Good morning to you, sir,' he added as we quickly left the pub for the street.

Once we were out of the pub and on the sidewalk, I asked, 'What's the hurry, all of a sudden? Did you spot McCreedy while my attention was on the Inspector?'

'Yes, I have seen him, Mr Mayne. I saw McCreedy arrive by hansom, but a few moments ago! That is the reason for the necessity of speed.'

'Are you positive, Mr Furst? Are you quite certain it was him? Where did he go?'

'I would recognise the shape and carriage of McCreedy anywhere. Besides, he wore a slouch hat like the one your sister described worn by the man who delivered the message that sent us to Andover. In addition, he was carrying what appeared to be rolled-up prints and a beautiful mahogany presentation box—probably the one my father had made for the two prototype pistols. He entered the same door as Mr Webley earlier. Let us give them a few minutes before we break up their meeting, shall we?'

Shortly, Inspector Morris and his companion left the pub, passing the two of us without saying a word or giving any other acknowledgement of our existence. We watched them walk away and observed their movements until they turned the corner. At that point, Mr Furst said, 'It is time.' He stepped off quickly toward the office building's entrance, and I followed close upon his heels.

Entering the building, we were met by the same security officer we had earlier observed. 'Hoy, there! What's your business here, now?' he challenged.

'We are here to see Mr Philip Webley,' Mr Furst said, 'on a matter of extreme urgency.'

'Is that so?' the guard replied. 'Well, Mr Webley is in conference wit a businessman, and he don't want to be disturbed. Come back another time, if you please.'

'We do *not* please!' Mr Furst shouted. 'We will see Mr Webley, and now! Step aside, or my man here will make short work of you.'

I did not expect a show of fisticuffs, but I tried to appear as foreboding as I could, pushing up my jacket sleeves and tipping my hat to one side of my head.

'I've a better idea, mate,' the guard said, sizing me up. 'I'm goin' to get the coppers, and then you'll be the sorry ones.'

'That is a terrific idea, my good man,' Mr Furst said, 'and make haste of it, as the trouble is about to begin.' With that warning and suggestion, the guard flew out the door, leaving Mr Furst and me to locate the meeting and stop the transaction. Several wood-panelled hallways with glass-windowed offices ran past the central guard station. Regardless, it didn't take us long to find Mr Philip Webley's office. It was the one from which loud voices were emanating.

Mr Furst and I listened outside the office in silence as the two men discussed the transaction terms and the sum of money to be paid. One voice was distinct and somewhat formal, while the other seemed agitated, quite American, and coarse-sounding.

'Mr McCreedy, the amount we agreed upon, I believe, was 500,000 pounds sterling, was it not?'

'The price, you cheap, double-dealin' limey bastard, was one million. As ye can see, it's all here, every detailed drawin'! And this here—look! Look at this beauty! They're only two pistols like this on Earth. You build these, and you'll be sittin' on top of the world, king of all gun makers, and you knows it, don't ye?'

'Yes, yes, I agree. These plans are incredible, and the pistol is most unusual and interesting-looking, but all I have to give you is 500,000 pounds for the lot in this portmanteau. Take it or leave it, Mr McCreedy. I must make you aware that I received a telegram from Superintendent John Rigby at Enfield late yesterday stating that you are a wanted man, very possibly a murderer, and two inquiry agents are chasing you. Further, he advised me not to do business with you if I met you. Therefore, sir, do you want the money in this portmanteau or not?'

'You know, I could use this on you and take the money and plans and be on my way without anyone bein' the wiser. Whaddaya think about that, your lordship?'

'I believe you to be a blackguard who is running out of options, McCreedy. Do anything as foolish as you propose, and England will be too hot to hold you. You shall receive the full measure of English justice. Mark my words, sir!'

At that moment, Mr Furst threw open the office door and stepped in, and I was right behind him. We both surveyed the situation, and I'm almost sure that Mr Furst viewed the scene with both trepidation and liberation, as did I. There, standing across from my friend, was the phantom of his chase. Although he wore his slouch hat low, I could tell how disfigured his face was, even with his heavy makeup. He was a hideous-looking man, but his deeds were even more hideous. What would happen next? I didn't have a clue.

'So, Captain Furst,' McCreedy, a smirk on his made-up face, said. 'after I set you on a long chase of me, we at last meet again man to man, perhaps for the last time, eh? I was hopin' that this day would never come, but here you are. Gave you a couple of slips along the way, eh?'

'McCreedy,' Mr Furst replied, 'you were a slippery one, I must admit, and it brings me no great pleasure meeting you under these circumstances. Know that I will always be grateful to you for saving my life years ago on that battlefield. Believe me when I say it pains me to see that your life has come to this—murderer, arsonist, thief, and confidence man. You and your partner, Mason, caused so much grief and suffering to so many in such a short time. For the sake of justice, now those conditions are about to change.'

'I don't reckon it will matter now if I admit to killin' Mason and Underwood, but it was all Mason's plan to kill your father and George before stealin' the plans and this here prototype. Captain, your father was good to me; he gave me a job when no one else would. And George, he was a likeable ol' Negro and never caused nobody no harm. But once we'd done the deed, there was no turnin' back. We figgered to make enough money off this lot, sail off to South America, and live like kings. But then, Mason got greedy, and I knew it was a matter of time before he got us nabbed if I didn't *lighten my load*. That's why I burned him. I'm sorry 'bout Underwood, but, well, I couldn't very well have him blabbin' off to the cops, could I? Now, it's time for me to leave you, Captain, either alive or dead—your choice.'

'McCreedy, if things had turned out differently between us, we might have become friends,' Mr Furst said. 'However, as it is, now I will be happy to watch you twist on an English gallows.'

'What about our deal, McCreedy?' Mr Webley pleaded. 'You received your money. Now, the plans are mine!'

'Mr Webley,' Mr Furst said, 'I am quite certain you would not wish to be known to the authorities as a man who was the receiver of stolen goods, would you? Those plans and gun are the property of the Furstenberg Firearms and Foundry Company, as evidenced by the seal on the schematics and the engraving on the pistol. In other words, they belong to me, the owner of the works. And now, McCreedy, will you come along with my partner and me peacefully, or must it be by force?'

'I'll not swing for my crimes, here or anywhere else! So, we are doomed to end this play as on the battlefield,' said McCreedy. 'Make yer move, Captain!'

With McCreedy's final words still ringing in our ears, Mr Furst thrust himself toward McCreedy, but not before the fiend had cocked and fired the prototype pistol he was holding. The gun made a slight bang sound, and Mr Furst reeled backwards from the bullet's impact and, grabbing his chest, fell hard against the wall.

As if in a dream, I was back on the grassy slopes of Majuba Hill, South Africa, in the middle of a raging battle. I drew my trusty service revolver and fired one shot in the direction of my friend's attacker. *Bang!* The bullet ran true and struck the would-be Boer assassin through his slouch hat in the forehead with a peculiar and sickening sharp metallic *clack*. The force of the strike was such that it threw the man back and off his feet, brain and blood splashing on the lush vegetation. I turned to take aim at the next Boer. It was then that I heard the sharp but painfully-forced command.

'Colour Sergeant Mayne, stand down!'

'Sir!' I shouted in reply.

Instantly, I was brought back to reality and saw that I was about to shoot Mr Webley, now white as a ghost. My hand trembled as I slowly un-cocked and re-pocketed my revolver. The command had come from my friend, Mr Furst, who was leaning against the wall and obviously in severe pain. Blood was oozing from the tear in his beautiful jacket just below and to the right of his left breast pocket. I rushed to his side.

'Steady on, old friend,' Mr Furst said. 'I believe I shall live—you have saved my life and won the day. Is McCreedy dead?'

I nodded. 'He is very much so.'

'Thank you for doing what I was hesitant to do, Mr Mayne. No doubt the police shall be here at any moment. I am certain Mr Webley will undoubtedly testify that you shot McCreedy in self-defense. Will you not, Mr Webley.'

'Well, umm, well, yes, I will confirm that fact to the police,' Webley said. 'And what of the plans and the prototype gun still in McCreedy's hand?'

'I am confident that the police will collect all of that as evidence, Mr Webley, and once they are satisfied the property is mine, will return it all to me, wherever I may be. I do not believe there is anything to be gained by my telling the authorities you were about to purchase stolen goods from a murderer. Do you?'

'Umm, no, I do not, sir,' Webley said. 'My sincere gratitude to you for that. Now, let us see to you.'

I gently unbuttoned his vest and shirt and examined Mr Furst's wound. I found several penetrations of varying sizes, depths, and severity. I had seen too many wounded soldiers in my life, and I was amazed the wound was not immediately fatal, given the shot's point of impact. McCreedy's aim, though thankfully not accurate, was damaging, nonetheless. The bullet had struck Mr Furst's holstered gun, causing it to shatter into several sharp pieces of shrapnel. I grabbed handkerchiefs from Mr Furst's pocket and from Mr Webley, adding them to mine. I then pressed the cloths into the wounds and attempted to stem the blood flow. I rebuttoned his vest to hold the makeshift dressings in place until my wounded friend could have a more suitable arrangement.

As expected, the security guard returned winded, accompanied by none other than a very tired-looking and angry Inspector Morris and his companion constable. Thankfully, they had travelled by police wagon and could load Mr Furst into it for his trip to the hospital.

'Mr Mayne, before they take me away, please secure the plans and prototype,' Mr Furst said before passing out.

Within a very few minutes, he was on his way. McCreedy's body would remain where it fell until the Inspector was satisfied with Mr Webley's account of the shooting.

As for me, I waited while Inspector Morris took Mr Webley's statement and gathered up the evidence. That task completed, the Inspector took me to the Steel House Lane Station to question me further about the incident in which I was McCreedy's killer. As the telephone was still out of order, I spent the rest of the day and night in a cell awaiting confirmation via telegraph from Metropolitan Police Headquarters in London of Mr Furst's and my identity and the case on which we were working. Luckily, ol' Granny came through, as I knew he would.

'I understand that you are a close personal friend of Chief Inspector Lestrade,' said Morris. 'How very fortunate for you. He vouches for you and your character. Further, from Mr Webley's statement, it appears you saved his life and that of your partner, Mr Furst. Therefore, I see no need to bother with the formality of assize or a magistrate in this case. You are free to go. Here is your pistol. By the way, I find it ironic that you saved the life of Mr Webley with your Webley service revolver.'

'Quite so,' I chuckled. 'What o' Mr Furst's property—his pistol, the one what McCreedy used, the mahogany box, and the drawings? It's imperative that I return them to Mr Furst immediately.'

'Normally, it would be entirely out of the ordinary to hand the property of another over to you, as you are not the owner. However, since you are Mr Furst's partner, I can see no reason not to. I will retrieve them from the evidence locker.'

Moments later, Morris returned with all for which I had asked.

'Thank you, Inspector Morris. You've been very kind. Can you tell me where Mr Furst was taken?'

'I had him rushed to Queen's Hospital, and I have been informed he is under the care of Doctor William Sands Cox, the eminent surgeon.'

'Excellent! Thank you very much. Good day, Inspector. I hope if we should meet again, it'll be under more pleasant circumstances.'

'Quite so, Mr Mayne.'

CHAPTER 16
CLOSING THE CASE – LAST DETAILS, WHERE TO GO FROM HERE?

I exited the police station with great haste and summoned the first cab I spied. 'Queen's Hospital, as quickly as you can, cabbie,' I ordered the driver.

Several agonizing minutes later, I was inside the hospital. At the front desk, I asked the matron about my friend, Mr Siderus Furst. After checking her records, the most proper lady reported, 'He is located in Ward "B," second floor, and you will please register with the nurses' station on that floor.'

I thanked the matron and sprinted, arms full of prints and the loaded mahogany box, up the stairs to the second floor to the indignant looks from the hospital staff. 'This is not the place for the darby, sir! Walk, please. No running in the halls!'

Nodding my assent but ignoring their recommendation, I continued my pace until I had reached my goal, the nurses' station.

'Excuse me, Sister. I am a friend of Mr Siderus Furst. Please tell me where I might find him,' I asked the young nurse sitting at her desk.

'Oh, yes, the wounded American. You are in luck. They have only just recently moved him from critical care to the convalescent ward. You will find him down the hall on the left and the second door on the right. Please do not stay long. Mr Furst needs his rest.'

I thanked the nurse and scrambled toward the door that she had stated. As I entered the ward, I saw a dozen or so beds close to each other on both sides of the wall. Still, it did not take long for me to locate Mr Furst. His artificial leg was standing at attention on the floor near the head of his bed, and the man, his torso and left arm bandaged, appeared to be sleeping.

Apparently, hearing me approach, he awoke with a start. 'Ah, Mr Mayne, it is you, my good friend. I was hoping you would come.' 'Of course! I came just as soon as Inspector Morris released me from jail. He received telegraphed confirmation from Scotland Yard about our identities, and he is satisfied that I acted in self-defense.

'What of Mr Webley?' Mr Furst asked.

'When I left him in his office, he appeared to be in a state of shock—staring at the bits of McCreedy's brain and blood splattered over the portrait of the queen on the wall where the fiend had fallen,' I said. 'If it was not such a dreadful sight, it would have been comical.'

'Ha, ha. Oh, my friend, please do not make me laugh. It hurts so.'

'Further,' I said. 'I brought all the items that McCreedy had in his possession. The gun is in the mahogany box, and here are the schematics.'

'Good, very good, my friend. Thank you. Come closer.' Then, in a near whisper, he said, 'I want you to find a private place and burn the plans and the box, as its insides hold the shape of the prototypes. Next, I want you to disassemble the gun and throw the parts in the closest canal or river. Will you do that for me, Mr Mayne? I will be even more grateful to you than I already am.'

'Mr Furst, you can trust that I'll carry out your desires entirely in secrecy.'

Just then, a doctor entered the room and approached us with a small pan. 'Ah, Mr Furst, it is good to see that you are alert and that you have a visitor,' he said.

'Doctor Cox, this man is more than a mere visitor; he is a friend, but more like a brother. May I introduce Mr Abaddon Mayne, the man who saved my life at Webley's. Mr Mayne, may I introduce Doctor William Sands Cox, the excellent surgeon who also saved my life in his surgery.'

We shook hands, bringing a broad smile to Mr Furst's now-scruffy face.

'Mr Furst, I brought this pan containing odd-shaped pieces of broken and twisted metal,' the doctor said, placing them on the nightstand beside Mr Furst. 'I removed them from your chest and arm. I have no idea what they are, but I thought you might like to keep them as souvenirs of your Birmingham adventure. You are very fortunate that your assailant's bullet struck whatever this was. As bad as your wounds are, the outcome could have been far more serious.'

'I cannot thank you enough for your skill, doctor,' Mr Furst said.

'You can thank me by staying put in bed for the next week. When your wound sufficiently heals for you to leave my care, I will discharge you as quickly as I can. Then, you may travel back to London for further healing. It was a pleasure meeting you, Mr Mayne. Please do not stay long. Your friend needs his rest.' With his final words of care, Doctor Cox left the ward.

'A week? In bed? Oh, Mr Mayne, there is so much to do!' moaned Mr Furst.

'Don't worry, my friend, I'll stay in Birmingham with you until you are well enough to travel by train, and then we both shall return to Dorset Street and Becky's delicious cooking. In the meantime, perhaps

I'll introduce you to Cadbury chocolate bars, which are made in this city. Does that strike your fancy, Mr Furst?'

'That sounds marvellous. However, in the meantime, what is the state of your purse, Mr Mayne? I know you are getting low on funds.'

'Don't worry about that, Mr Furst. I've made arrangements for such an occasion, and I will come to visit you every day. Then, if you are up to it, we might even play a few games of Brag.' As you may remember, reader, I had planned on using the gold pocket watch that my commanding colonel had presented to me upon my retirement from the Rifles as collateral against any lodging expenses we might incur.

'Now, about those "souvenir" parts—please dump them into the box and get rid of them when you dispose of the disassembled prototype.'

'You can count on me, sir.'

'I am confident of that, my friend. There are one or two more things I need before you go. First, please retrieve my cigar case from my jacket on the hook over there on the wall.'

'I don't think the doctors will permit our smokin' in the hospital, Mr Furst.' Still, I did as he requested of me. In his left breast pocket, I found the case, though quite damaged from the force of the devastating gunshot. I brought the once-exquisite silver case over to him.

'I am afraid it has passed serving its purpose as a cigar case, Mr Mayne. Regardless, please accept it as a small token of my esteem and gratitude. As you are aware, it has been in my family for generations. I cannot think of another soul I would more desire to have it. You have been as a brother to me. Even though we have been together for such a short time, you have shared my good times and bad, never leaving my side. I desire that the case be kept in the hands of family.'

My words failed me. I felt my eyes beginning to tear. Instinctively, I reached for my handkerchief, only to remember that I had used it on Mr Furst's wound. I hadn't felt an attachment to another soul since Tommy's death. Here, this American, a former stranger, called me "brother." Yes, I felt very much kin to the man lying before me. Even though we did not share the same blood, as Mr Furst said, we had shared the same good and bad times as intimately as any pair of siblings could. Again, I tried to speak but couldn't.

Mr Furst saw my emotional state and tried to make light of the occasion by playing down the gift. 'It is a trivial thing. Perhaps you could make a toothpick holder out of it. Or, you might straighten out the sides and use it to hold a deck of playing cards, eh?'

'Thank you, Mr Furst, for this wonderful gift. I'm overwhelmed, sir. I'll treasure it and our friendship forever.'

'As shall I treasure your friendship. One more thing, Mr Mayne, you will find a cheque for two thousand pounds, made out to you, in my pants pocket, also hanging on the hook with my jacket. Before we left for Andover, I wrote it but never had time to give it to you to cash before leaving London. Please use it to pay for whatever expenses are owed to you, your food and accommodations while we are here in Birmingham, and our train tickets home. If there is anything left, please give the remainder to your sister to replace the money she loaned to us and for my lodging at Dorset Street. If that is not enough, I will settle with you and her upon returning to London. I guess you will not have to pawn your gold presentation watch, after all. Eh, Mr Mayne?'

How did he know that pawning the watch was my backup plan? Would I ever be able to figure out the man?

'Now, Mr Mayne, I apologise, my friend, but I feel the necessity to sleep. When you return to visit tomorrow, we shall discuss our inquiry agency partnership in earnest.' With those trailing words, my dear comrade fell deep into what I hoped was a peaceful and healing slumber.

Who could suspect what adventures the coming weeks might bring?

The End of the Beginning

A BIT ABOUT THE AUTHOR

eM. Douglas Wade

Although born and raised in the Midwest, the author has spent the better part of his adult life living and working in New England. A U.S. Army veteran, he served in West Berlin in the 1960s. He lives with his wife, Barbara, in historic Stratham, New Hampshire.

He has written poetry, a prize-winning creative nonfiction story, and a prize-winning short story, but his passion has always been writing longer historical fiction. Wade received his Master of Arts degree in English and Creative Writing with a Fiction concentration from Southern New Hampshire University. Even though Wade has written two other novellas, *Furst and Mayne: Book I -- The Case of the Phantom Scarface Killer*, a Victorian crime-mystery-adventure work of fiction, is the first of its genre he has published.

Book Description

Boer War-tormented, retired British Army sergeant and story's chronicler, Abaddon Mayne, aids the relentless American detective, Siderus Furst, troubled by physical impairment and grieved by personal loss, in a race against time chasing desperate murdering fiends bent on capital crime in Victorian England. The two must stop the phantom maniac and his henchman before they can sell the stolen plans for weapons of unimaginable killing power to unwitting arms manufacturers. Will the patriotic duo prevail and save the world? Will justice and fair play win the day, or will the call for revenge consume the determined pursuers?